SHURIKEN SURRENDER

"Talk, you ol' buzzard, or that wet rawhide'll cut your gullet in two!" snarled one of the white men. "Just nod your head when you get ready to cave."

Realization chilled Ki, and he saw that a thong had been tied tightly about Shukka's bony throat. As the rawhide dried, it would contract and Shukka would be slowly strangled to death. And the old Indian would die before surrendering.

Something had to be done—and fast. A throwing dagger appeared in Ki's right hand, and he sent it winging toward the larger of the two men. The man cursed bitterly, and, ripping the dagger out of his thigh, he crashed limping into a fringe of timber.

Deserted by his compadre, the other man flung his pistol at the leaping Ki, whirled, and dived into the underbrush. . . .

DON'T MISS THESE
ALL-ACTION WESTERN SERIES
FROM THE BERKLEY PUBLISHING GROUP

THE GUNSMITH by J. R. Roberts
Clint Adams was a legend among lawmen, outlaws, and ladies. They called him . . . the Gunsmith.

LONGARM by Tabor Evans
The popular long-running series about U.S. Deputy Marshal Long—his life, his loves, his fight for justice.

LONE STAR by Wesley Ellis
The blazing adventures of Jessica Starbuck and the martial arts master, Ki. Over eight million copies in print.

SLOCUM by Jake Logan
Today's longest-running action western. John Slocum rides a deadly trail of hot blood and cold steel.

◆→ WESLEY ELLIS ◆→

LONE STAR

AND THE AZTEC TREASURE

J

JOVE BOOKS, NEW YORK

LONE STAR AND THE AZTEC TREASURE

A Jove Book / published by arrangement with
the author

PRINTING HISTORY
Jove edition / November 1992

ISBN: 0-515-10981-9

Jove Books are published by The Berkley Publishing Group,
200 Madison Avenue, New York, New York 10016.
The name "JOVE" and the "J" logo
are trademarks belonging to Jove Publications, Inc.

PRINTED IN THE UNITED STATES OF AMERICA

10 9 8 7 6 5 4 3 2 1

★

Chapter 1

Like a vast fortress hewn from a single block of stone, Malazo Mountain glowed in the white fire of the moon. South and southwest of the mountain, southern battlement of the Malazo Range, stretched the desert, an arid waste of sand and salt and alkali. Grotesque buttes and chimney rocks rose from its burning floor, and strange, symmetrical spires that almost seemed to be monuments set by man, instead of what they were—tombstones of ages long dead. Farther west were mountains, a purple shadow upon the Texas skyline, and farther to the south, beyond the Rio Grande, were other mountains, ink black against the dusky night—the mountains of Mexico.

The old Spaniards mined much gold and silver from Malazo's stony breast, legends said, but for hundreds of years no prospector ever discovered traces of precious metal in the Malazo Range. What wealth had been found stretched to the west and north of Malazo, where valley rangeland lay rich in grass and curly mesquite. And on the northern slopes of the mountains that formed the western wall of the wide valley were a few mines of value; their dark tunnel mouths gaped down at the cattle and mining town of Hope.

Flanking the Malazos ran the Malazo Trail, once trod by Coronado and the iron men of Spain, and immeasurably ancient when the Conquistadors first set mailed foot on the soil of Texas. Northward it rolled from the canyoned waters of the Rio Grande, veering slightly to the east across the fiery desert, up along the craggy foothills of the mountains, a broad ribbon of tarnished silver in the moonlight. Remote, lonely, desolate. Empty save for two riders on horseback heading toward Malazo's mighty slopes.

One was Jessica Starbuck, astride a travel-weary sorrel mare. Tall and lissome, in her twenties, Jessie wore a flannel shirt and denim jeans and jacket, all powdered with the gray dust of the desert, and a sweat-stained floppy-brimmed hat under which was tucked her long, coppery-blond hair. And despite an expression on her face mirroring the exhausting effects of her long journey, the night chill could not dampen the warmth of her sultry face with its high cheekbones, audacious green eyes, and the provocative if challenging quirk of her lips.

Close by her rode her companion Ki, on a tuckered Apaluche gelding as black as the soul of the night. He, too, wore typical rangeland garb showing signs of hard and long travel, with his hatbrim tugged low, visoring a lean face etched with deep lines of fatigue. In his early thirties, with bronze skin, blue-black hair, and almond-shaped eyes, Ki had been born to the Japanese wife of an American sailor. When orphaned as a boy in Japan, he'd trained as a samurai and become adept in martial arts.

Upon immigrating to America, Ki had been hired by Jessie's father, Alex Starbuck, head of the world-wide Starbuck business empire. Consequently Ki and Jessie had virtually grown up together, and after her father's murder it seemed only fitting for him to stay on, but as a loyal confidant to the young heiress. She took control of her huge inheritance and far-flung responsibilities, proving to be strong and capable, and harder than a keg of railroad spikes if need be. Working together, as close as any blood brother and sister, they made a formidable team.

Winding up into the foothills, they began discussing where they might camp for the remainder of the night. The prospects did not appear overly promising, for though they had passed from the barren desert flats, their immediate surroundings mainly consisted of stone and hardpan, the vegetation scraggly and scattered, with only occasional patches of pine and gorse and grass offering scant shelter. But camp they would have to, before their horses gave out, having ridden steadily all day and the day before from El Sabinas, the nearest stage depot, after an interminable trip across Texas from Jessie's Circle Star ranch. They'd had to buy the horses and gear, since El Sabinas' liveries insisted rental nags be returned in short order, but fortunately they'd found Jessie a tough, surefooted sorrel, and Ki had picked a black that had sand and bottom to spare.

And now, increasingly, came another reason for finding shelter soon. The full moon, having crossed the zenith and pouring a flood of ghostly light down the vast rampart of Malazo's western slope, was silvering the edges of storm clouds that rolled slowly up from the western horizon. On the dark breast

3

of the cloud bank was a flicker of lightning. The air quivered to the mutter of distant thunder.

Jessie glanced wearily toward the ominous clouds. "Along with everything else, Ki, it looks like we're in for a good soaking."

Nodding, Ki shifted his gaze from the approaching storm to the mountain slope, and his eyes quickened with interest. "Maybe not, Jessie," he replied, pointing. About a hundred yards above the trail was a broad bench well-grown with grass, stands of sotol, and bristles of thicket. In the face of the beetling cliff beyond was a dark opening. "Seems to be a cave, and from the looks of the grass and stuff, there ought to be water. I've a notion we could do worse than hole up there till the storm is over."

"Yes, and we still have some coffee, bacon, and a few eggs left in the saddlebags," Jessie said, eyeing the bench speculatively. "Suppose we take a try at it."

The bench was a hard scramble up the slope, but their horses made it without too much trouble. In front of the cave they dismounted, and Ki, breaking off a dry sotol stalk, touched a match to the splintered end. The sotol burned with a clear flame, providing a satisfactory torch. They approached the cave.

"Don't want to den up with a rattlesnake," he remarked.

Jessie shook her head. "No, nor with that big man-eating cougar that's supposed to be prowling hereabouts."

The floor of the cave, however, was clean and dry, and there were no signs of predatory occupancy. A trickle of water flowed along one wall, in a shallow channel, to lose itself amid the growth outside. Heartened, they unsaddled their mounts, picketing them to graze just outside the mouth of the cave. They unrolled their blankets on the cave floor, then gathered a quantity of sotol stalks and dead branches in the nearby thickets. Soon they had a good fire going, and shortly coffee was bubbling in a little flat bucket, and eggs and bacon were sizzling in a small skillet. With appreciation they sat down to a savory meal, which they consumed by the light of the fire, and to the music of the loudening thunder.

Afterward they cleaned and oiled their firearms, as was their custom and a damn good, even lifesaving, habit to get into in gritty, dust-clogging weather. In saddle boots they both toted Winchester .44–40 carbines—reliable, effective weapons in wide-open country. Jessie also carried a Colt pistol holstered on her right thigh, and a two-shot derringer hidden behind the brass buckle of her belt. Other than the carbine, Ki packed no firearm—he didn't care for them, as a rule—but he was far from defenseless. Sheathed behind his waistband was a short, curved *tanto* knife; and for a belt he used a *surushin*, a six-foot cord with a leather-covered ball at each end; and stashed in the pockets of his worn leather vest were slim throwing daggers and *shuriken*, little razored steel disks shaped like stars.

With guns ready to hand, they went to sleep to the accompaniment of rolling thunder and dashing rain. They did not sleep too soundly, but with one eye open and ears cocked for any unusual sound that might filter through the uproar outside.

It was an unusual sound that roused Ki shortly before dawn. He sat up, feeling greatly refreshed, and listened to a peculiar creaking and rumbling that drifted up from the trail below. The fire had died to gray ashes, but the storm had passed, and reddish light streamed into the cave mouth from the great globe of the sullen moon that hung just over the western mountain crests. Pausing for a moment, he glanced over at Jessie, who was beginning to stir in her blankets. Then he slipped to the mouth of the cave and peered out.

Along the trail, clearly outlined in the lurid light, crept a high, two-wheeled cart drawn by four sturdy oxen, and accompanied by a rider on a bay cow pony. Features hidden by the brim of a Stetson, the slim rider was either a youth or a young woman, clad from what Ki could see in buckskin-foxed riding breeches and a burgundy shirt. What appeared to be a peon of Mexican heritage, wearing a sarape and a straw sombrero, was hunched on the cart's drivers seat. The box of the cart was heaped high with something that gleamed in the waning moonlight.

"Salt cart heading for town," Jessie surmised with a yawn, joining Ki at the mouth of the cave. "My guess is it's been to the salt lakes to the east of here and's bringing back a load to sell."

Ki gave a noncommittal grunt and eyed the moon, the lower edge of which was now touching the western crags; it still wanted almost an hour till dawn. Turning back to his blankets, he settled cross-legged, crossed his arms and cupped his hands over his ears. He remained thus, relaxing and meditating. To a Westerner, his posture would have looked strange and uncomfortable; to a Japanese, it was a vital position for concentrating one's inner forces and reviving one's intrinsic energies, which were fundamental for health and strength. And Ki,

6

aware of the mission they were on, sensed that he would probably not have another opportunity for some while to come.

Jessie, too, relaxed. From the pocket of her jacket she drew a smeary scrap of paper upon which was an illiterate-appearing scrawl. Her brows drawing together, she read the disjointed sentences:

> Matt Beemis stay out of malazo country you aint wanted here and you aint got a chance in an hundred to git out alive we aint fooling
>   Quantrell

Jessie turned the paper over in her slim fingers, turned it over again, gazed at it with a thoughtful look. It had come to her at Starbuck headquarters two weeks before, clipped to a request from Matt Beemis, the on-site manager of the Twisted Bar, a Starbuck subsidiary ranch in the Malazo Valley. He had asked for help, and not only in dealing with "Quantrell," the writer of the threatening note. An extremely ferocious and wily cougar was preying on young livestock, and recently had turned man-killer. Also called pumas or mountain lions, cougars very rarely attacked humans unless cornered, wounded, or in defense of their cubs, but this maverick had for no apparent reason killed the owner of a neighboring ranch as well as the previous manager of the Twisted Bar, old Zeb Quale—as Jessie already knew; it was the reason she had appointed Beemis to the post. The cougar was terrorizing the region, and had so far eluded all attempts to track it down and kill it. Beemis wanted Jessie to send the best hunter available. Well, if Ki wasn't the best hunter around, he was right close to the top of the list.

Equally if not more troubling to Jessie was the rash of robberies and rustlings—many targeting the Twisted Bar—carried out by a cutthroat gang led by someone taking the name of Quantrell, the Civil War raider. Evidently the local authorities weren't faring any better catching the outlaws than they were the cougar, and Beemis's aggressive actions to stop the losses of Twisted Bar livestock were now proving to be a threat to him personally. And Jessie took it personally, as she did the affairs of all her operations and personnel. When she received Beemis's message, the note's warning scrawl had galled her. She had been about to cast it contemptuously away, when she noticed a peculiarity of wording and decided to keep it. And now, studying it intently by the gray light of coming dawn, she mused:

"Handwriting disguised, all right. Nobody who could write at all ever wrote this bad. And one little slip. Not much, but perhaps enough to drop a loop around some jigger's neck before the last brand's run."

The stillness was broken by their horses suddenly blowing through their noses, their ears pricking forward. Jessie folded the paper and stowed it back in her pocket, rose to her feet and called softly to Ki.

Ki opened his eyes and glanced inquiringly toward Jessie, now clearly outlined in the strengthening light of dawn. He sat up as the sound that had attracted their horses' attention reached them: a rhythmical clicking drawing quickly near—the sound of swift hooves beating the hard surface of the trail. Stepping to the mouth of the cave, Ki stood with Jessie well back in the shadow, and gazed toward where the trail curved around the mountain base to the south.

From around the curve bulged seven or eight hard-riding horsemen. Gigantic, unreal in the elusive light, the troop swept past, drumming toward the hills that were now bathed in a tremulous golden glow.

Jessie and Ki stepped forward and followed their progress with interested eyes until they disappeared around the next bend. Much of the trail from there on was lost from view as it twisted between bouldered clefts and through tree-studded thickets. Far ahead, though, some two miles or more distant, they could spot the salt cart and accompanying rider ambling northward across an open patch. They saw the rider and driver twist about and gaze at the approaching horsemen. Abruptly the driver faced front, and from the movement of his arm, they judged he was urging his shambling oxen to greater speed.

The racing horsemen swiftly closed the distance. Jessie uttered a sharp exclamation.

A puff of whitish smoke mushroomed from the ranks of the riders. Even before they heard the crack of the distant rifle, Jessie and Ki saw the ox-cart driver throw up his arms, pitch sideward from his seat, and sprawl motionless on the ground. The oxen stopped, turning their heads to look about. With one hand the accompanying rider struggled with a shying mount, while raising the other as though aiming a pistol. It was a futile defense; the horsemen charged forward with unabated speed, half reining in by the cart, half dragging the rider from the saddle, their assault so swift and furious that it was temporarily lost from sight in swirling dust. As the dust cleared, Jessie and Ki glimpsed horsemen roughly subduing the rider, while other horsemen swarmed over the cart, the salt misting through their hands as they scooped it up and flung it from the heaped-up bed.

With lightning speed, Jessie and Ki saddled their mounts and sent them skittering down the slope. Once on the trail, the clearing with the salt cart again lost from view, they leveled off to a smooth running walk, eager to close the distance as quickly as possible, yet without forewarning the murderous attackers of their approach. Manes tossing in the wind of their passing, eyes rolling, nostrils flaring red, their horses charged up the trail until, Ki estimated, they were roughly a hundred yards from the clearing, hidden only by one last blind curve. He slowed, gesturing for Jessie to rein in as well.

At the same instant, a new sound cut like a whiplash through the air—the shrill, terror-filled scream of a woman!

Quick pressure of their knees sent the horses into a thicket beside the trail. Ki leapt to the ground, Jessie an instant behind him, and tethering their mounts to trees, they snatched carbines from their saddle boots. Then, with soothing words to their mounts, they gained a line of scrawny conifers and went in a crouching run around through the timber toward the clearing. Gaining the shelter of a bordering thicket, they paused again to listen and get their bearings. The woman had not screamed again. Except for the harsh scolding of a blue jay, a deep, eerie silence lay over the area. But they were not fooled. They knew that a woman didn't scream out in wild fear or pain without reason.

Then, startlingly close, a man's venomous voice snarled: "Go ahead, Nick! Give 'er a taste. That'll make her talk!"

Instantly there was a sharp, hissing sound, followed by a pain-filled shriek from the woman.

The hair lifted at the nape of Jessie's neck, and quick, wicked anger slashed at her. She glanced at Ki, whose face was bleak as the granite of Malazo Mountain, eyes the cold onyx of a stormy winter sky. It was not the first time they had heard the snarling hiss of a whip as it cut through the air and bit into human flesh. Stealthily they moved forward through the thicket, those sinister sounds echoing in their ears. They heard a man laugh, a low, brutal sound, and heard the sobbing of the woman.

They hunkered at the edge of the thicket, which ran like a border along the top of a bank. Formed by an old landslide, the bank sloped sharply to the clearing below and was studded with boulders, stunted brush, and gaunt trees, as was a shallower rise on the far side of the clearing. The cart and oxen and the body of the driver were in the center of the clearing. The accompanying rider's bay and eight other saddle horses were grouped loosely, ground-reined, along the far side's fringe of grass.

But it was the stir of activity twenty feet from the horses that riveted Jessie and Ki's cold-eyed attention. Lashed upright to a weather-gnarled oak, her slender arms drawn forward about its trunk and tied on the opposite side, slumped an auburn-haired young woman in her early twenties—the rider who'd accompanied the cart, they could tell, by her buckskin-foxed riding breeches. Now she was hatless and shirtless, and her bare back was laced with livid welts. One breast was pressed flat to the tree, but the other, firm and perky, showed as she turned to peer over her shoulder, fear and agony in her wide hazel eyes. Behind

11

her grouped eight men, roughly dressed, gunbelted, their vicious faces stamped with the harsh brand of the out-trails.

One in particular stood out—huge, burly, his broad face slashed by thick, twisted lips and pitted with hooded black eyes that seethed with cruelty and violence. He was grinning wickedly at a gimlet-eyed, beak-nosed hombre who held a keen-lashed blacksnake whip in one hand; the muscles in his hairy arms writhed and bulged as he wielded the whip with slow, deliberate savagery. The whip made a wicked, snarling sound as it slashed across the quivering flesh of the bound girl's back. Her body jerked violently, and again she let out an agonized scream that trailed off into moaning sobs.

Savage, killing anger surged through Ki. Motioning to Jessie to stay put, he began snaking through the thicket to another vantage point farther along, figuring on catching the men in a crossfire. Jessie, realizing what Ki had in mind, remained low and cuddled the carbine butt against her shoulder, taking aim, impatiently waiting for Ki to get into position.

"Stop!" she heard the girl beg, whimpering. "Please . . ."

The big man with the hooded eyes lifted a hand. "Okay, Nick," he said, and when the man with the whip let it trail in the dust, the leader grinned at the girl. "Sure, sweetie, we'll stop. We ain't cravin' to hurt nobody. You ready to tell us what we're after?"

"I would if I could!" she pleaded, stricken. "But I can't!"

"You can, dammit! Your ol' man knew about Quetz—Quetzalcoatl and them there jewels, and it don't make sense he wouldn't tell you."

"Dad didn't! He—"

Swearing loudly, the big man turned back to the whipster. "The bitch is yours, Nick! You like blood, you like to tear folks to pieces and watch 'em die slow and hard. Get to it!"

The lash hissed as it uncoiled like a striking snake. Simultaneously, from the thicket, Ki's carbine blasted lead-fanged flame. As the carbine report rang out clear and metallic, Nick's arm, already driving forward to slash the whip across the bound girl's back, wavered and jerked downward. He tumbled headlong, slamming facedown against the ground.

Then suddenly so many things happened so fast that later Jessie was never able to put them together in a picture that satisfied her. She triggered just as the remaining raiders whirled, startled surprise making its pattern across their faces as they scrambled, plunging for cover. Some, including their leader, dove behind the salt cart; one bravo clambered up on a cart wheel to take aim at the brushy screen that concealed Ki. He reared smack-dab into the path of Jessie's bullet, and somersaulted off the wheel like a hurled sack of old clothes. Other men darted for the trees and boulders along the edge of the clearing, a couple of them springing toward the bound girl with the obvious intention of using her as a shield. Ki's carbine blasted again, and the couple split up; the one in the lead gave a queer, strangling cough and sprawled motionless, and his partner veered in a frantic leap into the underbrush.

The raiders, whittled now to half a dozen, tried to rally, sending bullets snarling waspishly up into the thicket, showering Ki with leaves and splintered bark, and slashing into the rotten log behind which Jessie huddled. But with the advantage of height and firing from separate angles, Jessie and Ki were able to keep the raiders fairly well boxed. The air above the clearing rocked to the echo of thunderous reports. A third outlaw reeled sideward, flopping and kicking, but he clawed to his feet again, a wild fear showing on his face as he stared upward toward the unseen shooters.

"I ain't standin' here to be slaughtered by thems I can't see!" he bawled, and scuttled like a giant crab on his wounded leg toward the horses.

His retreat was the signal for universal panic. Yelling and cursing, the surviving raiders fled wildly toward their plunging horses. Their leader swore bitterly, flung a last glance at the thicket, ran leaping into the saddle, and rammed steel to his mount. Hunkering within the thicket, Jessie aimed her Winchester at him, her greenish-gold eyes gleaming as she squeezed the trigger. She caught the man nearest the leader, when the leader zigged and the other man zagged at the last possible instant. The man toppled against the leader's horse, which shied and almost unseated the leader, who hurriedly slewed the horse about, out of Jessie's gun sights. Before either she or Ki could draw a bead again, the outlaw boss and crew had vanished into the underbrush and timber that rimmed the far side of the clearing.

Jessie sent a stream of lead crackling in pursuit. She had the satisfaction of hearing a wild thrashing and howling, but mainly from the distance came the rattle of hooves, fast diminishing overland out of range. She ceased firing, sprang to her feet, and raced down the embankment to the clearing. From farther along the thicket, Ki appeared and came rushing after.

The girl, unable to get free, had wisely flattened herself against the tree and hugged it, cringing, during the gunfight. Without speaking, Jessie drew her hunting knife and began slashing the girl's bonds.

Slowing slightly, Ki scanned the area for any signs of lurking raiders or ambushing guns. He saw none—but he remained suspicious, on guard. A single glance told him there was nothing to be done for the cart driver. The heavy rifle slug had torn through him from back to chest, just above the heart. Also, the three raiders they had downed weren't playing possum; they were lifeless bodies sprawled on the ground.

The girl, her back welted and bloody, stumbled slightly as the ropes were cut. Ki, pausing only long enough to collect her hat and torn shirt from where the raiders had dumped them, was just in time to help Jessie steady her, cradling her in his arms. She gazed up at them, trying feebly to cover her breasts with her hands. "Whoever you are," she managed huskily, "I owe you plenty, and I'm—"

"That can wait," Ki interrupted. "Those coyotes might get back their nerve and decide to circle back. Let's get up into the brush."

They hastened up the slope toward the spot where Jessie had lain, she and Ki assisting the girl. Moving deeper into the thicket, they found a spot where their position would be more advantageous in case the raiders decided to renew the fight. Ki went on, hurrying back down and around to where he and Jessie had tethered their mounts, and rather than taking the time to bring them, he grabbed the small kit of medicinals from Jessie's saddlebag and returned to the women.

By now Jessie had spread her jacket on the ground, and the girl was stretched out facedown, head in her arms. She craned to look up as Ki approached, gritting her teeth against the pain of the whipping. And Ki found himself highly impressed by her gritty determination, as well as by her nubile figure and freckled, snub-nosed gamin face.

"Miss Starbuck says your name is Ki," the girl remarked. "I'm Evelyn Rutherford of the Anvil, Ki, and . . . and thanks. Whatever your reasons for mixing in, I'm plenty obliged to y'all."

"Forget it," Ki said, smiling, and handed Jessie the medicinals. From the kit Jessie opened a small tin and began smearing ointment tenderly along the girl's raw welts. The girl stiffened in fresh pain.

"My God, that stuff burns like a branding iron!"

"It's arnicated carbolic salve," Jessie answered, pausing to quote the label: "The best in the world for burns, flesh injuries, boils, eczema, chilblains, piles, ulcers, and fever sores." She started smoothing it on again, assuring her, "Don't worry, it'll smart for just a minute, and then it'll just feel nice 'n warm. Evelyn, have you any notion who those attackers were?"

"I believe, Miss Starbuck—"

"Jessie."

"Jessie. And please, y'all call me Eve. Anyway, I believe it was Quantrell's bunch."

"Was Quantrell the big guy giving orders?" Ki asked.

"No, nobody knows who Quantrell is. To most folks in the section he's just a name—a name that's tied up with everything bad that's happened here in recent months, and there's been plenty. Besides, the big 'un kept referring to what Quantrell wanted and how pleased Quantrell would be that they'd

16

gotten two for one this morning."

"Meaning you and the cart driver," Jessie said.

"And it was all by happenstance," Eve added ruefully. "I ran into the driver and was just tagging along for company, though I must admit he didn't act too friendly. Still, it's a long trek to Hope from the Anvil." She gestured vaguely in a northwesterly direction. "The regular way is a little shorter. There's a track over beside the buttes that turns west from them a few miles north of here and crosses the valley by us. But I got up real early and took this route on the chance of meeting my foreman, Scat Vanion. He and some of the crew are down here somewhere. Yesterday they rode on the trail of a bunch that rustled a chunk of our herd and headed for the river."

"Odd . . ." Jessie frowned thoughtfully. "It doesn't seem reasonable for outlaws to throw down on a salt cart, and from the little we overheard, what they were torturing you to find out was even stranger."

"I know, it's absurd. The jewels of Quetzalcoatl!"

"D'you mind explaining?" Ki asked. "All I know of Quetzalcoatl is that he was—and may still be—a god worshiped by the Aztecs in Mexico. According to legend, the ancient Aztecs went through some kind of crazy rituals before golden images of this god, and offered up human sacrifices to it, mostly young girls. Quetzalcoatl was called the vampire god because he was supposed to live on the blood of these victims. But what about these jewels? And why would an old Aztec god be causing disruption up here in Texas?"

"There's more to the legend. At least, there is locally," Eve replied, a faraway look coming to her eyes as if she were seeing over unimaginable distances. "Almost a century ago, a party of American

17

adventurers are supposed to have made their way deep into Mexico, through the jungles to an Aztec temple on Lake Tezuco. There they slaughtered many Aztecs and stole a statue of Quetzalcoatl, a huge golden idol several times the size of a man filled with precious jewels. The story goes that a war party of Aztecs trailed the Americans and caught up with them somewhere hereabouts, killing some of them and retaking the idol. But the Americans regrouped and cornered the Aztecs who, slowed by their heavy idol, took refuge in the fortresslike hacienda of a Spaniard named Don Fundador. In the end the Americans wiped out the Aztecs, and discovered the Aztecs had killed to the last man, woman, and child Don Fundador's family and servants. The golden idol of Quetzalcoatl with its treasure was never found. Of course, that hasn't stopped rumors persisting."

"Or people searching," Jessie said. "Was your father out after it, or did he know or *think* he knew where to look?"

"No, of course not! The whole thing's ridiculous! And Dad would've set them and anybody else straight if he hadn't been killed by that mountain lion."

Jessie, thinking of Matt Beemis's message about the owner of a neighboring ranch falling victim to the cougar, almost blurted, *Oh, you're the one!* Swallowing the impulse, she said instead, "Ridiculous or not, Eve, Quantrell and his gang apparently figure your father was onto the treasure and told you its secret before he died. You're in danger until this is cleared up."

"What am I going to do?"

"First thing is to get you to a doctor," Ki responded, aware as Jessie was that the salve was

18

merely first aid treatment that would allow Eve to travel. Jessie was about finished, and thinking the girl wouldn't want him around while she dressed, he suggested, "If you two can manage, I'll fetch our horses and meet you in the clearing."

There was something else on Ki's mind—he had a hankering to check over the salt cart and driver. When he reached the clearing with Jessie's sorrel and his gelding, though, Ki first devoted his attention to the dead raiders. They were ornery-looking specimens, their distorted features lined by dissipation and the full rein that had been given to their evil passions.

"Typical border scum," he mused, "only some more intelligent-looking than the average. They weren't digging into that salt just for fun." Climbing onto the cart, he set out to enlarge and deepen the hollowed-out hole where its cargo had been scooped away. He had hardly begun removing the loose salt when his fingers struck something hard. He quickly realized that the heap that apparently filled the cart was in reality a layer only a few inches in depth. His groping hands got hold of a rough, irregular fragment of stone, and levering it out, he gave the stone one sharp inspection and called Jessie over.

By this time Jessie and Eve had come down from the thicket and retrieved the girl's skittish bay. Eve's burgundy shirt had been ripped into strips to fashion a bandage that now wound around her breasts and back, over which she was wearing Jessie's denim jacket. They hurried to the cart, where Ki handed Jessie the piece of stone, saying,

"I thought it was funny early on that the driver would be using four head of stock to pull his cart. Two is the usual number, and with water scarce as it is on this trail, no driver would take along animals he didn't need. What he was pulling is a lot heavier than a cartload of salt."

The stone was seamed and cracked and crumbly, and sprinkled through it, thick as raisins in a pudding, were irregular lumps of a dull yellow color. Also there were crooked "wires" crisscrossing the surface of the rock, and the fragment was astonishingly heavy for its size.

"Quartz," Jessie judged, staring at the fragment. "High-grade gold ore, with about the heaviest metal content I ever laid eyes on. If this cart is loaded with the stuff, and I imagine it is, it must be worth a big hatful of pesos. No wonder those men were after it, why they said they'd hit two for one."

Eve looked genuinely shocked. "Why, I'd no idea!"

Pursing his lips, Ki climbed down by the slain driver and turned him over on his back. To their surprise the man was not a Mexican peon of the sort that usually transported salt from the lakes. He was a hard-bitten Anglo with a straight gash of a mouth across his deeply tanned face, low cheekbones, pale eyes, now set in death, and a shock of hair of a peculiar dead black color that seemed to interest Jessie.

"Texan, and a miner, going by the calluses on his hands," she reckoned, and noted the lighter coloring of the man's sunken cheeks. "Used to wear whiskers, and they grew up almost to his eyes. Scrawny, but looks wiry. Packs a gun as if he knew how to use it. No salt freighter, that's certain, although he might be able to pass for one, especially wearing a sarape and with that sombrero pulled low, if nobody happened to look too close in bright light. Chances are that's why he shaved off his whiskers. Peons don't often have that much beard."

20

In the driver's pockets was nothing of significance. They were about to turn away when Ki noticed the corner of what looked to be a sheet of paper protruding from the front of the dead man's ragged shirt. He drew it out and, after studying it, gave it to Jessie.

It *was* a paper, of a sort, having the appearance of ancient sheepskin manuscript. Across its surface, stained with the slain man's blood, fine lines were drawn.

"Looks like a map," Jessie said. "A good piece of work, too."

"A map of what?" Eve asked curiously.

"Hard to say. Here, look it over. You know this country, and maybe you can figure something from it."

Evelyn Rutherford took the blood-smeared paper gingerly and bent her brows over it in the morning light. "It's surely a map of Malazo Valley," she said after a moment. "I recognize a number of things. Over here to the right is Malazo Peak with this trail. And see, way down here, the salt flats, and just up is Mule Ears Peak. It's marked plainly, a double peak that looks like a mule's ears. And the western range runs north and curves a little to the east, just as the Malazo Range runs north, only it drops away sharply to the east to widen the valley. But I can't make anything of these lines that crisscross the thing. I'm positive it's a map of the valley, though."

Jessie nodded, retrieving the map. "Yes, the mountain ranges are marked clearly. But the lines drawn seem to run every which way without making any sense. There's a key to it somewhere, of course, but unless you hit on that, the whole business doesn't mean anything. Just the same, I think I'll hang onto it. It might have a bearing on why the driver was gunned down—that, and what's in the cart."

Figuring much the same, Ki tucked the fragment of rock into his vest. "The nearest town is Hope, and it has a sheriff, doesn't it?" he asked, and when Eve nodded, he went on. "Well, he ought to be notified, and chances are he'd rather have the bodies left just where they are. But we'll take the salt cart along with us. Its load is a mite too valuable to leave down here unguarded."

While Jessie and Eve climbed into their saddles, Ki took a moment to untie his bedroll and cover the driver with his blanket, weighting it down with heavy stones. The three raiders he left as they lay. There was no difficulty in getting the docile oxen straightened and lumbering north along the trail again, drawing the creaking cart after them.

★

Chapter 2

The sun was low in the west when they approached
the sprawling cow town of Hope set in the shadow
of the western hills. Around them the valley, green
and amethyst, heavily grown with grass and boasting numerous groves, stretched to the beginning of
the lower slopes, where the transition from fertile
ground to arid was surprisingly sudden. From the
crests of rises the riders could catch an occasional
glimpse of the Malazo Trail, far to the east, winding wearily northward.

"Most of the mining is done up on that long slope
you can see over to the west," Eve explained to
Jessie and Ki as they reached the straggling out-
skirts of the town. "Lazarus is the biggest mine,
and they keep an office here. Perhaps they can tell
us something about that gold ore in the cart."

"Good idea," Jessie said. "We'll drop in on them,
after we get you to a doctor. Oh, and is there a hotel
we can stay here tonight?"

"Yes, the El Capitan Inn is all right," Eve
answered, and aware from what she'd been told
that Jessie and Ki were en route to the Twisted

23

Bar, she added, "Your ranch is really too far to travel comfortably tonight, I believe. And the hotel has quite a good restaurant too, if you wish. They're seldom filled up, except on payday nights."

Passing the town limits sign—which some wag had altered to read HOPE-LESS—they turned along a crooked main street lined with shops, saloons, and gambling dens. Roughly midway along stood the three-story hotel, boasting much plate glass and a false front emblazoned with EL CAPITAN in huge letters, looming up from a row of one-story shops like a festering thumb, its patch-painted siding looking like scrap lumber from some old dance hall.

As they passed, a buckboard drew up before the hotel and stopped. The driver was a slim, immaculate man who lent an air of elegance to his homely range attire. He had a thin, strongly featured face, a crisp mustache, and an aggressive tuft of beard on his prominent chin. His eyes were glacier blue, and seemed to have glint of derision in them as he turned to the passenger. The passenger had features of cameolike regularity, steady gray eyes, and black hair with a touch of gray at the temples. He was erect in bearing, broad of shoulder, deep of chest, and evidently of good height. His hands lay motionless on his blanketed knees, which from what could be seen were broad and muscular.

"It's Willis Diebold," Eve said in low tones as they jogged by. "That's his foreman, Olin Thayne, driving him."

"On first impression, Thayne's a little on the salty side," Jessie remarked, "but Diebold is a nice-looking gent."

"Yes, he is," Eve agreed, "and in a sense it's a shame. He was born here, I understand, but he left this country years ago. He came back six months back, shortly after his father died. Poor fellow, he's a cripple."

"A cripple?"

"Yes. His legs are paralyzed. He has to be lifted from the buckboard or chair or whatever, whenever he wishes to go anywhere. It's a pity."

Ki asked, "Has he always been a cripple?"

"No, I guess not," Eve replied. "He was injured some way a few years ago, I was told, I think he was shot. The bullet injured his spine. In any case, it's never made him bitter, although he doesn't say much. Men who work with him say he knows the cattle business. He keeps his Double Diamond ranch in fine shape and raises first-class beef."

In the alley at the next corner was a livery stable, where they stabled their horses and arranged to park the cart and oxen in the corral out back.

"Right across the street is Doc Kunkel," Eve said, indicating a small house of the sort called a "foursquare" cottage, with a doctor's shingle swinging in front of it.

Inside the front parlor, which served as an office, white-bearded Doc Kunkel looked up, his eyes narrowing a trifle, but he merely grunted when told of Evelyn's injuries. "C'mon, m'dear, let's have a proper look," he drawled, ushering her toward a rear examination room. "Thank your lucky stars for Miss Starbuck's prompt treatment. Sounds to me like you'll be right as rain in a jiffy, and probably not have a scar to show for it."

Pausing, Eve asked Jessie, "Are you going to the mine office?"

"No, first I think we should go see the sheriff."

"I'll meet you there," Eve said. "After all, I was part of it too this morning."

25

They gave her a quick glance, then left.

The sheriff's substation was a squat block building squeezed between a mercantile and a feed store. According to the chipped paint on the door, Sheriff Algonquin Gillette was in charge, and they found the sheriff inside, seated at a table, glowering at some reward posters. A rotund man, Gillette had a double chin, wore steel-rimmed spectacles, and smoked a smelly cigar. His brow wrinkled querulously as if he were bearing up under great mental strain, as Jessie briefly related the details of the encounter on the Malazo Trail.

"Smacks of Quantrell's hellions, okay," he declared with conviction. "Plumb meanest nest o' vipers in Texas, with no respect for wimmin, none a'tall. O' course, Bill Quantrell has been dead years and years—before you was born, Miz Starbuck— but folks still recollect the name."

"A way with the owlhoot brand," Ki responded. "To take the name of some notorious gent and try to live up to his reputation."

"This Quantrell is doin' a pretty good job of it, whoever he is," Gillette grunted. "Sort of a mysterious jasper nobody has ever seen before. Sometimes he's reported as wearin' big black whiskers; other folks swear he's clean shaved. Different folks who have tangled with his gang tell different stories."

"Could be more'n one of them," Jessie suggested.

"I thought of that," Gillette admitted. "Like the original Quantrell, let one hellion begin building a name, and others fall in and make out to be him. But each raid that's been pulled is enough alike to sort of mark 'em for the work of one gang. Naturally, different folks may spot different members for top dawg. But I figure there's some smart and salty boss directin' operations, all right. Well, I'll

26

ride down the trail first thing in the mornin' and collect them bodies. Right now I'd like a look-see at what's in that cart."

Locking his office, Sheriff Gillette went with Jessie and Ki back to the livery stable. The rheumy-eyed old hostler grumbled when he was ordered to fetch shovels, then watched them curiously as they headed out into the corral. Tossing the loose salt from the cart, Ki and Gillette revealed the clumsy bed piled with the valuable ore.

"Looks like Lazarus Mine ore," Gillette said, after carefully examining some samples. "Uh-huh, looks a heap like it, but I can't be sure. If it is, somebody is sure doin' a prime fancy job of high-gradin' up there. Wonder how in blazes they got it out and didn't get caught doin' it? They ride herd mighty close up there, and—Oh, howdy, Miz Evelyn."

Jessie and Ki turned to see Eve Rutherford crossing the corral from the stable. She was wearing a new shirt, an oversized red-and-black checked cotton that helped conceal the windings of gauze bandage protecting her back. She still walked a little stiffly from pain, but all in all seemed well on the way to recovery. "When you weren't at the office, I though you might've come here."

Sheriff Gillette gave an officious harrumph. "Very sorry to hear what happened to you, Miz Evelyn. How'msoever, I understand you were down thataway on account of Quantrell's gang running off stock from the Anvil. Why wasn't I notified?"

"I guess Scat and the boys didn't want to take the time," Eve replied. "Or perhaps they didn't think of it."

"Takin' the law unto their own hands!" the sheriff growled. "They'll get in trouble that way sometime. And I'd advise you to stay close to the ranch after

27

this, too. These owlhooters think your father told you where the Aztec idol and treasure is located, and you can't blame 'em much, considerin' the things your father said and the odd doodad he sported that time."

Jessie, recalling how Eve had stoutly denied that her father had known anything about the idol, glanced sharply at the girl and then asked the sheriff, "A doodad? Did Mr. Rutherford have a piece of the treasure?"

Gillette, oblivious to Jessie's glance at the girl and Eve's embarrassed reddening, waved an arm and explained, "Don't know if the doodad was or not, Miz Starbuck. Lester—Mist' Rutherford—only showed it once I knowed of, a coupla months ago in the Sapphire Saloon. Happened to be standin' next to Les when he took it from his pocket and placed it on the bar. Plain enough it was some kind of jewelry. The saloon was crowded, and at least fifty men saw the thing." Gillette gave Eve a rueful look. "No disrespect intended, but you know how after your mother died, Les took to drinking. And sometimes in his cups, he was reckless and talked too much." The sheriff turned back to Jessie and Ki. "Wal, Les bragged about knowing where there was plenty more like his doodad, and said something' about what sounded like Quetzalcoatl. I rec'lect somebody saying, 'Hell, that's a piece of old Aztec jewelry! Where'd you find it?' But Les Rutherford kind of clammed up then and put it back in his pocket, and he wouldn't talk no more."

"He never would," Eve admitted glumly. "I heard about it, and asked him about it. He was sober then and denied the whole thing. Then one evening about three weeks ago Dad left the ranch and didn't come back. Scat found him next day, mauled by the

28

cougar." She gazed up at the sheriff, blinking back tears. "But how could anyone believe him, his windy yarns? I don't know where he got that thing, but how could he have found any Aztec idol or treasure? How could he have gotten past Shukka and his followers?"

"Y'got a good point." Gillette stroked his chins, then answered Jessie's and Ki's questioning looks. "There's a strange band of Indians outta Mexico living in this vicinity. It's rumored they were originally Aztecs who came up here after their lost god Quetzalcoatl, although this's never been proven, who've intermingled with the local Apaches. Well, their village still lingers in the foothills near Chuacas Canyon, a few miles to the west of here on the fringe of what's now Anvil property. The ruins of Don Fundador's hacienda are just inside the canyon. Ol' Shukka leads 'em, and they stick to themselves, hostile to strangers. Les might've owned the land, but he wouldn't have gotten to scrounge around much without a major fracas."

With no more to be said, they reburied the ore with sand, bribed the hostler to silence, and left the livery. Sheriff Gillette insisted that Eve Rutherford accompany him to his office to look over Wanted posters, on the off chance she'd be able to identify her attackers. Again she paused, glancing over at Jessie and Ki.

"I'd rather not ride to the Anvil alone after dark," she told Jessie. "Would you mind registering me at the El Capitan, and we'll all leave together tomorrow morning?"

Jessie was pleased to agree. Willis Diebold and his foreman were no longer in front of the hotel, nor were they to be seen in the busy lobby or adjacent restaurant and bar. Not that Jessie cared one way or the other; she was just gratified to be able to rent the last three adjoining rooms available, and to arrange for their traveling bags to be fetched from the livery. She and Ki then walked to the Lazarus Mine office at the far end of town—a cramped plank-board cabin which, according to the lettering on the door, also served as an assay office open to the public.

Inside, the man on duty proved to be the Lazarus Mine superintendent, sourly filling out paperwork at a rolltop desk. A middling-sized man with middling features and a humungous handlebar mustache, he examined the fragment of ore with keen attention.

"Appears like some of the rock we've taken from high-grade pockets," he said finally, "but I can't be sure without comparing it carefully with specimens known to come from the Lazarus. Not that there's much doubt about it in my mind," he added quickly. "There's no other ore like this produced anywhere else in the section. I'm just making the point that we can't claim that cartload on the mere assumption it's from our mine. We'd have to establish ownership definitely, a thing difficult to do under the circumstances. Tell you true, though, what interests me more'n the ore is how the devil it got took from the mine without being detected. We keep a strict watch on our high-grade, believe you me."

"Looks sort of like an inside job," Ki suggested.

"It certainly does," the super agreed, his mustache bristling. "And it will be my urgent business to find out how it was done. I'll hang onto this specimen of ore, if it's all the same. I have to work late tonight, but I should find the time to analyze it."

It had now fallen dusk, and they returned to the hotel in mind of a good meal. Entering the restaurant, they found a table and gave their orders to a white-aproned waiter, then looked the place over with interest. Although there was a fairly sizable dinner crowd scattered around, most of the occupants were cowhands patronizing the barroom section, drinking, eating at the free food counter, bucking the roulette wheels or the faro bank, or absorbed in poker. As the darkness deepened, numbers of miners in muddy boots and red or blue woolen shirts trooped in. Local shopkeepers and workers were also in evidence.

What intrigued Jessie and Ki more was the sprinkling of men who wore rangeland garb like cowhands, but who, Jessie decided, were not.

"Some hardcases long on twist," she remarked.

Ki nodded. "I've a notion this joint is a sort of stopping-off spot for gents on their way to the border, or the other way around."

As they ate, they were conscious of more than one sideward glance cast in their direction. Evidently strangers came in for a careful going-over. It indeed struck them that there was a tenseness about the place, a furtive air of suspicion, held in leash but nevertheless apparent. As if nobody was quite sure of his neighbor.

"Reckon no one is certain if the man standing next to him may be Quantrell or one of his outfit. Well, maybe this might smoke one out," Jessie said, and took the blood-smeared map of Malazo Valley from her pocket, spreading it under the light of the table lamp. "Besides, I want a closer look." As she bent over it, her brows suddenly knitted. In the strong light she saw what she had missed in the morning dimness. Almost obliterated by the

31

blood smear were tiny letters. With some difficulty she spelled them out: V of Malazo to Lazarus—Malazo W.

"What can you make of this?" she asked Ki, showing him the writing on the map. "It must have some meaning."

Ki examined the map, shaking his head. "V of Malazo to Lazarus—Malazo W. It doesn't make any sense to me." He then restudied the lines drawn on the paper and concluded, "Well, at least Eve Rutherford's right in her guess. This's undoubtedly a map of the valley. The hills to the west, the wide upper portion, the narrow neck that leads to the desert, with Malazo Peak here at the southern tip of the Malazo Range . . . And here, look, Jessie, I bet this tiny circlet on the slope west of town designates the Lazarus Mine."

"Perhaps it points out the route that should be followed by whoever lifts the ore from the mine," Jessie suggested. With a baffled exclamation, she refolded the map and put it back in her pocket. "But the lettering sure has me guessing. No, it doesn't seem to make sense, but I've a hunch it's the key to the whole thing."

"Y'know, we could show the map to the mine superintendent and see if he can figure anything of it."

"Good idea, Ki. Let's give him a try. He said he'd be working late."

They sauntered out of the hotel, appearing casual but keeping a sharp eye peeled for anyone following them. Spotting no one, they turned up the quieter side street on which the mine office was located. They were pleased to note a dim glow shining back of the dusty windowpanes. They went around front, and Jessie had raised her hand to knock when they saw that the door stood nearly half-open.

Stepping ahead of Jessie, Ki leaned forward and glanced inside, seeking the superintendent's desk. Then with bewildering speed he hurled himself back, shouldering Jessie aside. A revolver blasted, and a slug hissed past his face and sailed across the street.

"Stay down, Jessie!" Ki warned, recovering and whipping out a throwing dagger just as a shadowy figure leapt forward and swept the lighted lamp from the super's desk. Darkness blanketed the room, through which gushed lances of reddish fire. The walls rocked to the roar of revolvers. Twisting, writhing on the floor, changing positions each time he tossed a dagger, Ki answered the blazing guns as best he could. Bullets smashed the floor around him, knocked splinters into his face, thudded into the walls. He felt one rip his sleeve, another whip the side of his head. There was a clatter of breaking glass and spintering wood.

Leaping up in pursuit, Ki collided with a body, slashed out with a knife. He heard a man grunt in pain. Then fingers like rods of nickel steel bit into his shoulder, and he was hurled aside with prodigious force. He staggered, reeled, pitched over an unseen chair, and hit the floor with a crash. Before he could regain his feet, there was a second clattering of glass, followed by a patter of swift feet outside the smashed rear window.

"Ki!" Jessie cried out. "Are you—?"

"Yeah, I'm fine," he called back. "Don't come in yet."

For tense moments Ki lay where he had fallen, listening intently. The room was still save for a mumbling mutter over to one side. Finally he got

33

cautiously to his feet, listened, took a chance, and fumbled a match. He struck it, held it at arm's length an instant, and dashed it to the floor. The quick flare had shown him he was alone in the office save for a huddled form that moved feebly against the far wall.

Ki risked another match. The desk lamp was smashed, but there was a bracket lamp on the wall nearby. He touched the match flame to the wick, and the room was bathed in a soft glow. By now Jessie had rushed in, and together they hurried across to the prostrate man on the floor and turned him over on his back. He was the superintendent.

The super opened his eyes and stared blankly at them bending over him. Another moment and he fully regained consciousness. They helped him up and guided him to a chair.

"I dunno what happened," the super mumbled, in answer to their question. "I was working at my desk and turned around when I heard a sound behind me. Got a glimpse of two masked men."

"Handkerchief around the lower part of the face?" Ki asked.

The super shook his head. "Nope, their faces was completely covered, 'cept for eyeholes. I'd hazard they had the masks, black they was, strapped tight around their heads. Nary a chance to see their features—only the glint through the holes. Then one hit me over the head with something—a gun barrel, I reckon. Don't remember nothing else."

"You have a knot on your head, but I don't think it's anything serious," Jessie said, after a swift examination. "But they certainly made a mess of your office."

Which was decidedly not an overstatement. Drawers had been jerked out, their contents dumped and thrown about. A filing cabinet had been emptied on the floor, adding to the scatter of papers off of the desk. As Ki searched about, collecting his throwing daggers, from outside came a sound of shouting, drawing swiftly nearer. A moment more and boots pounded on the boardwalk. Several men rushed into the office, with Sheriff Gillette in the lead. He glared suspiciously at Jessie and Ki.

"What in tunket's going on here?" he demanded harshly.

They and the super told him, briefly.

The sheriff asked, "What were they after?"

"Sure beats me," the super grunted, peering around. "There's nothing of value ever kept here. We don't even have a safe. I was just going to give that ore fragment a check with my microscope when . . . Say, where is that chunk, anyhow? It was right here on my desk."

A thorough search of the office failed to uncover the fragment.

"Reckon one of the robbers pocketed it," the super finally concluded. "Well, it don't matter. You can get another specimen from that cartload, can't you?" he asked, turning to Jessie and Ki.

Jessie nodded, her eyes thoughtful.

The sheriff swore, apologized to Jessie, and asked Ki, "You get a look at 'em?"

"Not much. About all I saw was the blaze of a gun before the light went out. They sure threw lead fast for a minute, then went through the rear window."

"Big hombres?"

"I figure one was pretty sizable, Sheriff, from the way he took hold of me," Ki said. "Had a grip like a bear trap."

"Too bad you ain't armed. Mayhaps you could've downed 'em."

Ki didn't bother to correct the sheriff, feeling disgusted enough about missing them with his knives without broadcasting it. Evidently he hadn't even connected solidly with the one he'd taken a swipe at; there were no blood spots anywhere.

"Wal, there's a chance they got scratches goin' through the glass. That's something to be keeping an eye open for—not that the hellions wouldn't have an alibi for it. I reckon they got plenty of savvy." He nodded to his companions. "C'mon, you fellers. We'll look the ground over outside and see if we can pick up a trail. Reckon they vamoosed down the alley." He asked the superintendent, "You okay?"

"Oh, I'm all right, aside from a headache," the super replied. "I'll start cleaning."

"We'll lend you a hand," Jessie offered, and turned to the sheriff. "While you're hunting, would you stop at the livery and pick up another hunk of that ore from the cart?"

" 'Pon my word, ma'am, and I'll bring it right here."

After the sheriff and his men left, and Jessie and Ki had helped the superintendent straighten his office somewhat, Jessie broached the subject of their visit.

The super took the map and studied it. "This's the valley, okay, but that seems to be all. Let's go over it with a glass and see if we can find anything more." But a careful scrutiny of the paper revealed nothing more, the glass merely corroborating Jessie's translation of the minute letters beneath the bloodstain. "And what that means is anyone's guess," the super said. "I've a notion your supposition is right—it plots the route to be taken

36

by the high-graders, only it doesn't show where they go after leaving the valley. Mexico, I suppose. Easy to dispose of the ore down there."

Jessie nodded, but said nothing. The concentration furrow was deep between her brows, a sure sign that she was doing some hard thinking.

"Well," the super said, "things are in pretty good shape again. I think I'll go home. My head don't feel so good."

They left the office together. At the next corner, where the superintendent had a room in a boarding house, Jessie and Ki said good night, then continued along the main street, discussing the night's events. They had just reached the swinging doors of the Ace Full Saloon when Sheriff Gillette came barging out, wiping beer froth off his lips and looking much disgruntled.

"I was hoping to run into you two," he declared. "Couldn't find hide nor hair of the hellions, I'm afeared. We combed the whole town. The alley back of the office twists and turns among the shacks and 'dobes the miners live in and there're plenty of holes they could've slid into."

"Didn't figure you'd have much luck," Jessie remarked.

"And worse luck yet, the cart is gone."

"Wha-at?"

"Yep, them oxen is grazin' in the corral, but there ain't no cart there or in the stable or nowheres else I can see."

His listeners stared at him, then with one accord hurried to the livery stable. In the stable, the rheumy-eyed hostler was stretched flat on his back in a hay pile, snoring something insufferable, an empty whiskey bottle beside him. His clothes and the surrounding hay were drenched with water,

37

showing the futile attempts by Sheriff Gillette and others to rouse the hostler with bucketfuls of water.

"Dead drunk," Gillette snorted disgustedly.

Another search was instigated, with barren results. The cart was indeed gone from the corral and stable and everywhere in view. Requesting that a lantern be brought, Ki hunkered and studied the broken sod of the corral with keen eyes, then went over to a section of the pole fencing and examined the poles and the dirt around both sides.

"It was taken out here," he concluded. "You can see the wheel marks plain, crossing from where we parked it and through to the rear field beyond. Some scuffing shows here, too, where the poles rubbed the posts when they were dropped loose. Also, there are prints of horses' irons."

The sheriff said something under his breath that certainly was not fit for a lady's ears. Aloud he remarked, "That load must've been almighty valuable for 'em to've taken the chance on sneaking it away from here."

"Yes," Jessie agreed quietly. "Chances are, a lot more valuable than we had any notion."

Ki glanced at her quickly, but Jessie did not see fit to elaborate on her cryptic remark. The sheriff, glowering out at the dark field, grumped, "We'd never be able to trace 'em at night out over that hardpan and rock. Dunno if I'll have any better luck come light, but I'll give it a whirl."

Returning through the stable, Ki paused beside the sleeping hostler and picked up the empty whiskey bottle. He sniffed it, then wet his lips with the few drops left. "Laudanum," he said, spitting it out. "No wonder the guy won't come to. Somebody likely left the bottle handy, and he grabbed it like

38

a present from heaven. He'll think it was from hell, tomorrow."

"Well, I can't help envyin' him right now," the sheriff remarked glumly. "It's past time for all of us to snatch a li'l shut-eye."

Jessie and Ki offered no objection to the suggestion, and they left the livery together. At the hotel, Sheriff Gillette bade them good night and headed for his office. Having collected their keys at the front desk, Jessie and Ki ascended to their rooms, which were simple, utilitarian, each with a cast-iron bed, a mirrored bureau with a basin and pitcher, and a single side window with the drapes pulled closed.

Entering her room, Jessie lighted the milk-glass lamp on the bureau, locked the door, and made sure the window was firmly latched. Then she pulled back the covers of her bed. Her gaze fixed on the white pillow, and held. Pinned to the pillow slip was a fragment of smeary paper. Across it was penciled a rude scrawl. Jessie's eyes narrowed as she read the two words: GIT OUT.

The writing was indubitably the same as that in the warning note to Beemis folded in her pocket . . .

In his room, Ki had not yet locked the door when there was a knock and Eve Rutherford slipped inside. "No, Ki. You cannot stay here, not after all that's happened today," she said with a shudder. "Come with me."

"But—"

"Come with me," she insisted, in a tone that brooked no argument.

What the hell, he thought, and obligingly followed as Eve swished down the hall in her floor-length peignoir nightgown. Ushered into her room, which was exactly like his and Jessie's, he asked, "Okay, now what?"

"Now what?" Eve locked the door, smiling coyly. "Now we go to bed."

Ki regarded the short, narrow bed. "Why, Eve," he said in mock surprise as she moved closer, "are you suggesting we sleep together?"

"Is that so awful?" she murmured, scrutinizing him with her luminous hazel eyes. Her chin was raised and her uptilted face was yearning. "You saved my life this morning, and I'm very grateful, personally very grateful."

Ki was growing interested, but he was also growing worried about playing her game. He wondered how far she'd tease, how far was *too* far, and he didn't care to face any more uproar tonight. "Eve, you don't have to—"

"I know." She laid her hands on her chest, palms flat, fingers kneading. "I want to." She pressed her body against him, her arm circling his back and clinging as she kissed him for a long, burning moment. Ki responded with enthusiasm, kissing her back, feeling her lips clinging hungrily, her breasts mashing against his chest, her hands shifting to rub along his hips.

They broke for air, but she continued to grip intimately, stretching on tiptoe. He untied the ribbon at the throat of her gown and then began to unhook the little clasps of her bodice. "Damn," he growled, fumbling. "The sleepwear some females have . . ."

"You one of them perverts or something?" Eve laughed a little and opened all the rest of the clasps herself. "Sleepwear's made to be taken off," she added lightly. Shrugging her shoulders, she slipped the gown off and let it blossom around her feet, exposing a smooth, unblemished midriff, pointed breasts topped by raspberry-sized nipples, and a plump pudendum, with lips accentuated by a thin line of velvety curls. There was no sign of bandages, and whether by intent or accident, when she sat down on the edge of the bed, she kept her back with its healing wounds out of view.

Aroused, Ki hastened to be rid of his clothes. Eve stretched out nude on the bed, watching him strip with that vacant, burnt expression some women got when they're ready for sex. She was breathing hard, as though there wasn't enough air in the room, when, naked, Ki lay alongside her on the bed and gently embraced her. His hands moved impulsively, spreading tenderly across her flat stomach and up over her perky breasts. Trembling from his touch, she shuddered and gripped him, pulling him, urging his hand to slide between her legs and along her sleek inner thighs. Her hips slackened, widening to allow him access while she kept murmuring in a low, passionate voice, "Take me, take me, take me . . ."

But Ki was not ready to take her. He dallied first in the delights of sexual foreplay. He licked the curve of her neck and the tiny lobes of her ears, then lower, nuzzling and kissing one breast at a time. His groin pressed against her pubic bone, and he began pumping his jutting erection along the sensitive crevice between her thighs, yet never quite penetrating her.

Eve opened and closed her eyes, gasping and whimpering. Her buttocks jerked and quivered, her legs rolling and squirming until they were splayed out on the sheets, and she whimpered as though in pain, arching her body.

"Oh, your poor back," Ki whispered, hesitating. "Sorry."

"Don't tease me, Ki," she mewled, rolling over. Then, climbing on top of Ki, she undulated as she gently lowered herself, slowly enveloping his turgid length until she squatted, her pubic bone pressed against his. And then she jumped, impaling herself on him forcefully as she came down. Ki gasped. She hovered above him, thrusting with her hip and buttock muscles, pumping on his hardened girth until the bedsprings squealed in protest, blissfully ignoring her wounds and pummeling Ki with increasing abandon.

Thrusting in rhythm to her frenzied tempo, Ki sucked one swaying breast into his mouth, flicking her distended nipple with his tongue while grasping her other breast with his hand. Her passion continued building to an insane pitch. She writhed and wriggled and squirmed in a dozen different directions. Ki felt his excitement mounting higher, and sensed he was on the brink of release. Her auburn hair was a dizzying cloud in his eyes, the tang of her sweat was on his tongue, her dilated gaze glowed with ecstasy as, together, they hammered at yet a faster pace, pushing deeper, their sweating bodies slapping and rubbing tempestuously.

"Come! Come with me!" Eve pleaded loudly, as he felt her inner sheath contracting spasmodically from her erupting belly—and Ki climaxed with her, spurting deep up inside her milking belly. And long after they were both good for nothing, Eve was still wailing, "Come with me, come!"

"Enough," Ki said. "Whoever's in the room next door will think I'm beating you."

She calmed down and fell against him, stretching her legs back so she could lie with him inside her. "Yes, yes I suppose. But Ki, oh, how I wish . . ."

"What?"

"There's madness going on in this valley, a madness that's taken my father and the cart driver, and is threatening to take everyone else, too. I wish I could stop the madness, but I can't. I must do what I can, must make the best of the life I have here . . . I must make the best of you, Ki . . . In a while, again in a while . . ."

Sighing, she fell asleep.

Ki lay awake beneath her, meditating for a time afterward.

★

Chapter 3

Jessie, Ki, and Evelyn Rutherford left Hope at sunrise. To the west were mountains, blue and purple against the morning sky, their crests touched with flame, little more than five miles distant from the cow and mining town at the head of the Malazo Valley. As they progressed southward, the flanking slopes on their right veered slightly to the west, then fell away sharply as the curve of the valley widened, until in the northwest they were shadowy with distance. To the east ran the Malazos, almost a solid wall of stone, with the towering bulk of Malazo Peak forming their southernmost tip.

And between the dark walls, a good thirty miles in breadth, was a great grass-grown and wooded cup, shimmering like a cluster of emeralds in the sunlight. After a long stretch of riding down-valley along the wagon road from Hope, they came upon a narrow lane that cut away to the right. Nailed to a peeled log beside the lane was a large wooden signboard carved with the Twisted Bar brand and the name TWISTED BAR RANCH * A STARBUCK ENTERPRISE. By now the sky had lost some of its sunny brilliance, and on the horizon was an edging of pale gray, sluggish clouds, dirty and slightly folded, looking much like stagnant scum.

Angling off the main trail, the three riders took the Twisted Bar lane across a patch of rocky knolls and then through pocket meadows dotted with cattle. Soon, across a grassy field, they saw a line of cottonwoods, indicating a creek. It was another fifteen minutes before they spotted the ranch proper, fronting that creek. There was a big barn, a bunkhouse, a cookshack and mess, a smithy shop, and several corrals grouped around the main house.

Having hitched their horses at posts by the main house, they stepped to the porch and Jessie rapped the brass knocker on the front door. After a moment the door swung inward, Matt Beemis himself answering the knock. For a moment Beemis stared at them. Then he grinned with welcoming recognition.

"Miz Jessie—and Ki, b'gawd! And Miz Evelyn! C'mon in!"

Jessie hadn't seen Beemis in a good four years, but however he'd changed over that time, it wasn't noticeable. Roughly ten years older than she, he was still darkly tanned from the sun, lean-hipped and bowlegged from hours in the saddle, and toted his same old Starr .44 pistol like a tool, ridiculously high on his hipbone. As Jessie recalled, though, Beemis happened to be a wizard with a rifle.

Closing the door after them, Beemis ushered them down a corridor, commenting soberly, "Thanks for coming, Miz Jessie." A handsome man in a craggy way, he had a lopsided nose and a generous slash of a mouth cut for good humor. It had quirked pleasantly when greeting Evelyn Rutherford, but now it lost its amusement.

Jessie was his boss and not here for fun. "I apologize and take full responsibility for allowin' things to slip so bad outta hand here."

"Please call me Jessie," she replied, hoping informality would ease his strain. "And don't blame yourself for faults not your own, Matt. Zeb Quale always claimed your best *was* the best, especially after you took over as top hand here at the ranch, under his management. That's why I had no trouble deciding to promote you in his place. He said you two worked together as closely as equal partners."

"He said that of me?" Beemis rubbed his jaw. "Did he tell you the time him 'n' me held off a whole dozen rustlers?"

Jessie nodded, deadpan. "He said he was caught on a barbwire fence and couldn't run, while you had your gun snagged and were forced to shoot through your trouser fly."

Beemis looked in imminent danger of exploding. Suddenly he relaxed, however, and his anxiety dissolved into hearty laughter as they entered a tidy workroom and ranch office. A battered rolltop desk stood near the window. There were several chairs, big ledger journals, and wall-length shelves lined with books—including a large number of highly technical works dealing with geology, petrology, prospecting, practical mining, and similar scientific subjects.

"Yep, them were Quale's," Beemis said as he sat down, noting Jessie scanning the books. "Zeb was always interested in many topics other'n livestock and ranchin'. Ki, the puma that got poor ol' Zeb is plenty smarter'n the average cat. If you can run it to ground, I'll be right proud to hang your trophy right here over my desk."

"No question it was this particular cougar?"

"If you mean were there witnesses, no." Beemis rubbed his jaw again, thoughtfully. "Well, there may've been one, but nobody's seen him since."

"How's that?"

"The night afore Zeb died, he came home from town with a stranger, a gent he introduced to me as Burt Ander, a prospector. Looked like one, too, a shabby, gray-bearded sourdough. Anyhow, him an' Zeb sat up all night gabbin', I dunno what about, and early next morning they rode out together. They could've parted company a while later, or Anders might've panicked seein' what happened to Zeb and hightailed for the hills, or who knows what. But nobody's glimpsed hide nor hair of the galoot since, not even after the word went out for him two days later, when the boys found Zeb, what was left of him, on the west range beside a spring. 'Twaz an awful sight, the front of him torn to shreds, mauled face to foot. Oh—excuse me, Miz Evelyn. Didn't mean to upset you."

"N-no, that's all right. It just reminded me of the way my f-father looked when he was brought in," Eve managed, looking faint. Before fully realizing what she was saying, she added, "What a terribly painful way to die. I know, from what little I experienced."

Beemis turned ashen. "The puma attacked you?"

"There're other ways of getting slashed raw," she replied, and after an embarrassed hesitation, she revealed the whipping she'd received—and why. "And that's how I met Jessie and Ki," she concluded. "That's how come they're escorting me to the Anvil."

Beemis, his face flushing with rage as he listened, balled his hands into anger-trembling fists.

"This's gettin' beyond bearin'! It's not bad enough that our herds are decimated by rustlers and that damn puma, menfolk and now not even women are safe anymore! Wal, sooner or later we'll bag that cat, but I suppose we'll always have outlaws with us, and be forced to deal with 'em in the same ways."

"With a gun and a rope?" Jessie asked mildly.

"Yes," Beemis said, his eyes darkening, "but I prefer the methods of law and order. That's what we need more than anything else—good law enforcement."

"What's wrong with Sheriff Gillette?"

"Oh, Gillette's okay, Jessie, but I fear his ability is limited to plenty of courage, strict honesty, and a fast gun hand."

"Good things, all of them," Ki remarked, "but none of them a substitute for brains."

"And brains are what we are up against here right now," Eve said soberly. "Brains joined with courage, fast gun hands, and *dis*-honesty."

"Well, Quantrell and his gang ain't all that brainy, either," Beemis said, eyeing the girl. "Not if they're chasing this foolish—if dangerous—rumor about the Aztec god and hidden treasure. Plumb daffy, of course, but the legend seems to have just enough basis in fact to keep it going. Periodically for almost a century this treasure hunting fever has broken out like a rash, and now this! For no reason!"

"What about the piece of jewelry Lester Rutherford showed in the bar?" Jessie asked.

Beemis shrugged. "Maybe it was Aztec, like somebody said. Les made frequent trips to El Paso—he could've picked the thing up in a second-hand store. And much as I hate to say it, when Les was in his cups he liked to boast and act mysterious." He glanced ruefully at the girl, as though his remarks about her father might have wounded her, then asked as though to make it up, "Say, would it help if I tagged along with y'all to the Anvil?"

"It isn't necessary, Matt," Jessie responded. "I know you have plenty to do right now, and when Ki and I return this evening, we'll have time then to go over details. In fact, I think we should be riding on now . . ."

A little later, Jessie, Ki, and Eve Rutherford headed back along the lane to the wagon trail. For a mile or two they rode practically in silence, and then Jessie remarked to Eve, "I do believe Matt Beemis would've liked to come along very much."

Eve's eyes danced. "Poor dear, he fancies he's in love with me."

"Fancies?"

Jessie glanced around. Ki stared straight ahead, wooden in his saddle. Eve colored, dropped her gaze, and changed the subject.

They had covered perhaps three-fourths of the distance to the Anvil when Eve gestured to a large white ranch house set on a hill to the left. "That's the Double Diamond *casa*—Willis Diebold owns it. Ahead and to the west is the Forked S, a spread that lost a lot of cows just last week. Jason Ribeiro owns it. To the east yonder is the Scab Eight, Ron Goulart's spread. Then comes the Laddered V and the Sixty-Six . . ."

Jessie and Ki listened, with little comment, as Eve chattered on about the valley and its inhabitants. Ki in particular was continually studying the terrain, missing nothing, as the wagon trail they were following turned more to the west. Before

50

them rolled the valley rangeland, seemingly endless, green blotched with cinnamon and gray where the grass had been scorched by dry summer heat. The air was completely without motion. It was almost noon when Ki took another look at the sky, his first good look for many hours.

He didn't much care for what he saw. The scum of clouds that had once skylined the horizon had now overtaken them, having accumulated overhead slowly and so lifelessly that its growth was almost imperceptible. They were in for rain.

They reached the crest of a wooded rise, and the Anvil ranch house and other buildings lay before them in the near distance.

"The spread runs from the desert ten miles north, and from this rise west," Eve informed them.

"West to the mountains?"

"Farther than that, Jessie. Our western line is the far slope of that big ridge. Dad obtained title to the Anvil from the state. Later he included that section of the hills, why I don't know. They're nothing but a pile of rocks where nothing will grow. The canyons, and there're lots of them, that cut this side of the ridge provide shelter from storms and heat, of course, but otherwise the hills are worthless so far as anybody has ever known. And if Dad had some notion about them, he never explained."

"Is Chuacas Canyon in there?" Ki asked thoughtfully. "And that hacienda where the Aztecs were wiped out and the idol disappeared?"

Eve nodded. "The hacienda is on what was once the eastern fringe of a huge rancho, part of a Spanish grant awarded Don Fundador. The don was a tyrant, so the stories go, a wicked man who had grown rich on loot he had taken from Sonora missions—but that is not important now. As I say, the ruins are still there, deserted except for bats and snakes. The Indians and Mexicans call it *El Rancho de Sambres*—Ranch of Ghosts—and from my few visits, I can see why. It's a wierd, shivery place, especially at night."

They angled off the wagon trail, descending the rise through squat brush yellow with flowers, and shortly entered a tree-shaded yard. In and around the yard was a normal amount of clutter and equipment; along with a clapboard barn and a smattering of sheds, there were a substantial pole corral holding some horses, and a large pueblo-style house, flat-roofed, with beam ends jutting from its thick adobe walls and a gallery running the front length of the building. As they drew near, they observed a man pacing back and forth along the gallery with short, jerky strides.

"It's Sheriff Gillette!" Eve exclaimed. "And something's bothering him. He always prances that way when he's put out about something."

A few hands were working on this or that, and one of them hurried over to take their horses as the three dismounted by the gallery. Sheriff Gillette waited for them, looking very irritable indeed.

"Are you plumb loco?" he snapped at Jessie.

"Can't say for sure," she returned evenly. "Guess I'll have to leave that to other folks' judgment."

"If you leave it to me, I'm of mind to answer yes," the sheriff said. "Thought you told me there were four corpses for me to look over down there on the Malazo Trail at the edge of the desert!"

"Come to consider, I believe I did."

"Well, you're either loco or you was seein' things! There sure ain't none down there now. Nary a one,

52

much less four! You sure you didn't make up that yarn you told me?"

"Sheriff Gillette," Eve cut in frostily before Jessie could speak, "remember I also saw them, and ask Doc Kunkel if I haven't proof I was there!"

The sheriff glared at her in turn, an expression of personal injury on his face. "Well, they sure didn't get up and wander."

"No, I'd say somebody must've taken them."

"But what the devil for, Miz Starbuck?"

"So nobody hereabouts could get a good look at them. Maybe Quantrell and his men were scared someone would recognize their dead pals and tie them up with somebody else," Jessie suggested. "Seems to me that would also explain why the two men who raided the Lazarus office last night were wearing full face masks—it's the sort of stunt pulled by outlaws who're known around their area, maybe seeming to lead decent, even respectable lives."

The sheriff looked at Jessie, his brows wrinkling querulously, but quickly settling as the notion sunk in. "B'gawd, I believe you're right! Sorry I flang off'n the handle, Miz Starbuck, but things have been worse and growin' worser in my bailiwick, and I've been at my wit's end."

Jessie thought she heard Eve murmur, "That's not very far," but she wasn't sure as the girl spoke up, "I didn't recognize any of the attackers, Sheriff. I don't even remember what any of them looked like, things happening so fast and me so frightened and all. Sorry."

"Reckon that's natural, but I sure wish you hadn't been so hysterical," the sheriff remarked gloomily. "Well, womenfolk are womenfolk, and there ain't no changin' 'em. Reckon I better be headin' back to town, before the hellions wideloop the jail. Ain't nothing safe hereabouts anymore . . ."

After the sheriff departed, Eve Rutherford ushered Jessie and Ki into her parlor. A fat, middle-aged woman shuffled in and was introduced as Bertha, the housekeeper and cook; Bertha promptly declared that a luncheon snack was in order and assaulted the kitchen with a frenzy.

By now it had begun to drizzle, and the rain was thin but chilling. They watched it through the windows, the drizzle increasing to a shower by the time Bertha summoned them to the dining room for a "snack" that would've ruined many a restaurant. Table talk was kept casual, a bantering diversion from the looming threat of death and destruction, while outside the rain turned steady with drops like fat grapes, no thunder or lightning or threshing of wind, just a heavy, sodden down-pour. It passed on quickly, however, the overcast gliding southeasterly and the sky clearing over-head about the same time as dessert was served.

A clatter of hooves sounded outside. Eve sprang to her feet. "Here comes Scat and the boys!"

She ran lightly to the door, onto the gallery, and down the steps. Jessie and Ki followed her, gazing at the ten horsemen who were dismounting in the ranch yard. Rain-soaked they were, splashed with mud, a bunch of husky, hard-featured, saddle-worn waddies, packing handguns and toting carbines in saddle boots. They looked frustrated and discour-aged, rankled and uncomfortable from being so wet, and eyed Jessie and Ki—especially Ki—with gazes of mingled distrust and curiosity.

Eve introduced her foreman. Scat Vanion was tubby but muscular, turtle-jawed, with a bald spot on the front of his otherwise long-haired skull. He looked Jessie and Ki up and down as his crew had, with hard, suspicious eyes, but his hand was cordial enough.

"We didn't catch up with 'em," he told Eve, referring to their pursuit of the rustled cattle. "We didn't catch a sight of 'em."

"Scat," Eve said, "we can't stand much more of this with the obligations we have to meet."

"I know we can't," Scat replied grimly, "but what in blazes to do? They hit here, they hit there, and are gone like shadows into a dark canyon. We can't set a guard on every beef that's amblin' the range—every beef, that is, that the mountain lion don't get. That's right, Miz Evelyn, on top of everything else, that lion killed another of our young heifers." Scat indicated one of the crewmen. "Raoul here reported finding it to us on our ride in, so we detoured over and salted the carcass with strychnine, just in case the lion returns to feed. Fat chance! No mortal can bag it. It's a beast sent by Satan, that's what it is, to plague the souls of us sinners."

"Oh, come now," Eve said somewhat testily. "It's bad enough having to listen to all the local poppy-cock about Aztec rituals and Quetzalcoatl living on the blood of human sacrifices, without you adding more nonsense about a devil cat wreaking damnation."

"I'll keep my peace, Miz Evelyn. And I'd agree with you that it's tripe, if I hadn't seen that lion with my own eyes." The foreman gave a shudder.

Eve sighed. "Well, dry off and chow down, boys, you deserve a rest. Jessie, I want to thank you and Ki for escorting me home. This afternoon I think I'll ride over to the Forked S and Double Diamond, and if there's time, swing by the Laddered V. I want to find out if any of them have gotten a line on Quantrell, and to talk over the possibility of a roundup next week or so. If you're not in a hurry to get back to the Twisted Bar, you're more than welcome to accompany me."

"Thanks, I will," Jessie accepted. "It could be informative."

"I'd like to go see the carcass," Ki said. When Vanion cast him a startled glance, he explained, "Well, I'm sure if there're any cat tracks, they've been washed out by now. But looking over a fresh kill might give me some idea as to the size and age and so forth of this cougar. And seeing how it kills might even provide a clue as to why it's stopped stalking its usual prey. Wild animals sometimes turn man-killer due to an injury or infection that slows them down."

"Okay," Vanion said. "Raoul, ride Ki out there."

Raoul was sinewy, with gaunt protruding cheekbones and a white-pitted throat, and was the most taciturn puncher Ki had ever met. Perhaps he was peeved at having to ride back out instead of eating and resting, but if so, he didn't show it. He showed nothing, and said nothing the entire trip.

The carcass was near the western edge of the Anvil range, in a pocket thickly grown with tall brush. Obviously the cougar had dragged the heifer there from wherever the kill had taken place out in the open and, after eating, had covered the remaining carcass with dirt, leaves, needles, and bits of wood. This behavior, Ki knew, is innate in most solitary wild cats, and is intended to hide the food from other animals and keep it fresh until the cat returns in a day or so to feed again. What was a little odd in this case was that there were paw prints visible in the rain-softened earth around the kill. The cougar had returned much earlier than Ki would've normally expected.

The cougar had not fed again, however. Ki was not surprised. From studying the clean, efficient way the cat had killed—by grasping the heifer in its sharp-taloned paws and using its powerful jaws to break the neck—Ki figured the cat was a skilled, experienced adult, who in its wariness picked up the scent of man or poison or both, and left untempted by the easy meal. The size of the paw prints confirmed that the cougar was full-grown—oversized, even—and after surveying the pattern of prints for a while, Ki thought he detected that the cat had the broader-haunch stance of a female. But that was just a hunch at this point.

"I appreciate you taking me out here, Raoul," he said at last. "You can return now if you want, and tell the others that I'm going to see where these tracks lead."

The puncher finally reacted. He raised an eyebrow and drawled, "You ain't loco enough to hunt that cat by y'self, are you? Why, man, we done sic hounds and all after it, and all we's gotten for our trouble has been Johnny McDorn's pride bluetick bein' chomped dead. We actually treed the fuckin' critter once, and it jumped from the upper branches to another tree like some rabid-arsed monkey, and then down 'pon us. Shit, did that cause a consternation amongst us dawgs and men!"

"Well, I'll take a chance while I've got the chance—not that I expect to catch up with the cat, much less catch sight of it."

The cougar was easy to follow at first. The rain-sodden sward reached knee-high, and the trampled grass had not straightened when released by the cat's padding feet. From the pocket, Ki saw the tracks leading across the range, like a sign-board arrow, pointing clearly westward to the wild, mountainous hills. But even if the trail proved to be as simple to read in the hills—which it assured-ly would not—Ki had no illusions about catching the cat by himself. With its keen eyesight and hear-ing, the cougar would be well aware of him long before he could spot it. The best he could hope for was to locate the cougar's den, most likely well hidden somewhere up among the rocks—but even that was a poor possibility, for a cougar could claim a territorial range of two hundred miles.

With the end of the grassland, Ki had to ride slower, scanning the surface of the increasingly stony hardpan. Working higher, he found the hills dark and craggy, slashed by canyons and gorges, their slopes either bristling with stunted timber, or too rocky and devoid of moisture to afford root-hold to large growth, although thickets were in evidence from time to time. As expected of so elusive an animal, the cougar had avoided open spaces and run between walls of brush and boulders that were higher than the head of a mounted man.

Often as not the cougar prints vanished alto-gether, lost among the naked rock and hard earth crumblings that shifted, impressionless, under pressure. Ki would have to dismount then and walk his horse as he studied his surroundings, listening for any significant sound. Eventually he would discover a paw print or some other sign, such as marks on a fallen tree where the cat had sharpened its claws. Mostly he went by trust, a com-bination of knowing the line of travel already taken and sensing where it would most likely continue. It wasn't intuition, and he wasn't a bloodhound; it was solid logic, long experience, and putting himself in the position of the cat. That was the advantage of tracking an experienced animal or human. A greenhorn dude was unpredictable and difficult to track, once he'd gotten out of sight. But a mature cougar's behavior was forever dictated by innate wildness, and it could be trusted to do the instinctively logical thing at every turn.

After again losing the track for some time, Ki saw the prints reappear in the richer loam of a sloping field. He traced them higher. The path continued close to the contours of the hills, rarely up along the ridges, but down through clefts and gullies. Moving on, he had to rein in twice more to survey the terrain, deciphering the route as it wove among the spurs and timbered banks. As last he entered a narrow culvert and, while scanning the rimrock, glimpsed a wink of sunlight reflecting off something metallic.

He flung himself from the saddle, just as the report of a rifle shattered the early afternoon silence. A bullet whispered past his head. Tumbling prone behind a boulder, he winced as the rifle cracked a second time and chips of granite flew in his face. Then there was silence, a malevolent stillness.

Now it had become a stalking game, Ki realized. Whoever had waylaid him would wait him out— or try to. How the ambusher had known Ki would be coming along, or if he'd been lying in wait for somebody else or nobody in particular, Ki had no idea. Didn't matter. Irregardless, the attack was a fact, and Ki had no more intention of letting the ambusher get away with it than the ambusher had of letting Ki get away alive.

From his initial glimpse and the subsequent puffs of powder smoke, Ki was sure of the ambusher's location. Cautiously he began working his way toward the slope, darting from stone to stone, keeping as much as possible behind cover. In the silence, the least noise carried. Ki thought he heard a foot scrape rock, and tensed, waiting and watching . . . then began easing slowly to higher ground again in a long, curving detour that would bring him around above the ambusher, on the ambusher's blind side.

Approaching, Ki flattened, forcing himself to go more slowly and gently than ever. Again he caught the sound of a foot scraping against the rocks. Once more he tensed, listening, realizing that the ambusher was creeping closer, as though moving to a different vantage. The man was definitely trying to act like a snake, slithering and slouching behind rocks; but he was nervous, edgy, not always placing his feet as quietly as he should.

In such a situation it was understandable for men to grow anxious and twitchy. But Ki grew merely more icy and calculating. He was hunting a vicious sniper, but purposely employed the same cunning and techniques he would use stalking a savage four-legged man-killer such as that cougar. Noiselessly he inched forward, his nimble fingers feeling the razorlike *shuriken* blades that were tucked in his vest pockets. He heard a soft grunt and, aiming for it, listened for more sounds to home in on, until finally he eased into position and stared over, downward.

A man hunkered behind the low rockery of a small ledge, crouching on one knee while sighting a Spencer .56–50 repeater, tensing, preparing to blast anything that moved below.

Rising, Ki ordered, "Lay it down."

The man pivoted, firing as rapidly as he could lever.

Ki nailed him in the heart and throat.

The ambusher toppled awry with his leg bent under him, his rifle still gripped in one hand, the points of two glittering *shuriken* protruding from his chest and neck. Ki paused, ready to hurl another *shuriken* if need be, then gingerly made his way down the embankment to the ledge and stood over the prostrate, dying figure. And a little shock went through him. The ambusher was an Indian—Apache, most likely—dressed in faded drill pants, calico shirt and hide moccasins, his long, raven-black hair held in place by a crimson bandeau.

"Who are you?" Ki demanded. "Why'd you try to kill me?"

The man choked, grimaced in pain, but did not reply.

Staring, thinking, Ki realized his first impression was wrong. The man was not Apache. Some Apache blood, but not much. He was too big for an Apache, and his features were too smooth and regular.

Ki hunkered, leaned close. "Who are you?" he insisted. "*What* are you? You look a lot like an Aztec!"

The man shuddered, his chest heaved once, and he expired, twitching a final tattoo on the stony earth.

"Hell!" Disgusted, Ki turned away. Inspecting the dead man's Spencer, he found it was a stock '65 Indian model without oddities or markings that might provide clues. There was no sign of a horse anywhere around that Ki might check. Frustrated, perplexed, he stood a moment longer on the ledge, mulling over implications. There was small doubt in his mind. He had seen Aztecs deep in Mexico, and here before him was a man with Aztec blood in his veins. But why had the Indian tried to ambush him?

Ki's gaze lifted to the dark, timbered heights not far away, remembering Sheriff Gillette's story of the strange tribe that, supposedly, had come up out of Mexico. Their village—or that of their descendants—would have to be somewhere relatively close by, perhaps only a few miles away.

Eager excitement stirred inside him. He lifted the dead Indian in his arms and clambered up the embankment, where he located a shallow niche in which to lay the body. Then he placed rocks over it to protect it and returned to his horse. He mounted and rode on at a faster pace, deeper into the hills.

★

Chapter 4

All Ki had to go on was Eve Rutherford's vague explanation of the area—that somewhere in this general vicinity, along the eastern flank of these mountains, were the Indian village, Chuacas Canyon, and the old hacienda. Once he was out of the culvert, however, he saw the path. He noticed it by chance, and could easily have missed it, the path being no more than a single-file ribbon where passing hooves had beaten the ground raw. But that meant people had been riding the path more or less regularly, and that meant it had to lead someplace that was inhabited.

Turning, Ki jiggered his horse into a trot. The path wound higher through brush and timber, rocky gulches and flinty hogbacks, and presently, emerging on a ridge, he glimpsed a pale drift of smoke rising from the hills beyond. It was scarcely more than a wisp, yet it was sufficient to confirm that somewhere yonder, someone was burning a cookfire.

From there on the terrain grew increasingly rough. Canyons gaped unexpectedly. Gaunt slopes loomed on all sides, some timbered, others like the hairless spines of huge prehistoric monsters. For years this desolate country had been the stamping grounds of marauding Apache and renegade whites. Prospectors and adventurers had roamed its wilderness, seeking its fabled lodes of treasure—and many times finding death, instead. Above towered the mountain ramparts, frowning, hostile, majestically beautiful in their barren grandeur. Through their hidden passes had trooped early Spanish explorers in their quests of the mythical Seven Cities of the Cibolians.

After some while Ki came to a rushing white-water mountain stream that cascaded its way down through the hills. Both he and his mount drank their fill, then followed the path deeper into the hills. Finally, passing through a belt of timber, he reined in abruptly. The Indian village lay before him, sprawled between the rushing stream and a line of towering red cliffs.

Unlike most Indian villages, this one had a distinct orderliness in the arrangement of the adobe huts and hide-covered hogans. At the base of the cliffs Ki could see the entrances to several caves, which obviously also served as living quarters for the Indians, for half-naked children played about the openings. In addition to the children and dogs, more than a score of adult Indians were visible at various points about the village. They were staring at Ki, and he knew that they probably had been aware of his approach moments before.

He spoke softly to his horse and rode forward, slowly but without hesitation. Riding past a group of squaws and gaping children, looking straight ahead, he threaded between two rows of hogans and approached the center of the village. Here a group of bucks, dressed much as the ambusher had been, lounged in the shade of a huge oak and silently watched him. At ten yards, he reined to a halt. These Indians, he noted, had the same regular, coppery features as the one he had killed. They stared at him, not stirring, their black eyes cold with hostility.

Placing his hands carefully on the saddle horn, Ki returned their stares and tried to remember the name of the ancient chief. "I come as a friend, an *amigo*," he said slowly at last. "I would like to talk with Shukka."

For a moment he thought that the Indians had not understood him. Then one of the bucks turned without speaking and walked slowly toward a hogan that was the largest in the village. He disappeared through the doorway, and Ki waited expressionlessly, not looking at anything in particular. The buck reappeared at the hogan doorway, standing respectfully aside to let another pass. This second Indian came without hesitation straight toward Ki. He was incredibly old and scrawny, his thin shoulders stooped, his bare arms like crooked reeds. Yet despite his age the old one walked with a quick, springy step.

He stopped within a few feet of Ki. His parchmentlike face was a network of wrinkles that looked as ancient as time itself, but his eyes, set in deep pits, were alert and intelligent. "I am Shukka," he said in almost faultless English. "No stranger is welcome here."

"My name is Ki. I bring news."

"What kind of news?"

"An attempt was made on my life from ambush," Ki said slowly, gesturing back the way he had come. "I was forced to kill my attacker. He was one of your people, a tall man."

There was a moment of dead silence. Shukka's expression remained unchanged. Then one of the Indians muttered a single word: "Hopelchén!"

"I buried this man, Hopelchén, under some rocks to keep away vultures," Ki said softly, and he explained exactly where the body lay. "I am sorry, but I will kill any man who first tries to take my life—"

"You go!" Shukka cut in harshly. "Do not return!"

"*Bueno*." Ki's lips tightened, irritation stirring inside him at the old Indian's imperious order. But he knew that this was neither the place nor the time to start a ruckus. The young Indians were watching him, fingering their guns, awaiting only a word from their old chief to spring into action.

Reining his gelding around, he slow-walked back out of the village, knowing that to show fear or bolt might bring a hail of lead after him. Indians, good or bad, respected courage. As he reached the timber, still at a leisurely pace, his annoyance cooled. After all, he *had* been trespassing, and perhaps the ambusher, Hopelchén, had just been overeager in protecting his tribe. Hopelchén—that was an Aztec name. Ki's eyes narrowed in thought. More and more he was becoming convinced that in the story he'd heard there was considerably more than legend.

He made a half circle through the timber, returning to the stream about a mile above the Indian village. In his ears was a steady droning roar that was louder and more deep-throated than the usual rushing of water over rock. More like a waterfall, Ki thought—and paused in amazement as he broke through a screening thicket into a small clearing.

Before him was a rock wall, and spouting from

66

a hole in the rock was a solid, living stream of foaming water. Here, Ki realized, was the source of the stream that fed the village, springing cold and clear from the bosom of the earth itself. The fissure through which the water tumbled was perhaps five feet across. The water came with a surge and a roar, plunging downward ten feet into a deep, clear pool. Here, he realized, was a miracle of nature— a torrent of pure, sweet water flowing from the earth's breast to sustain life in man, beast, and plant.

His gelding tugged at the bit, seeking to drink again. The horse had not sweated excessively, so when he pulled, Ki gave him his head. The horse drank, siphoning the cold water in long, audible gulps. And Ki, relaxing in the saddle, suddenly looked without believing. At the side of the pool, not more than a few feet from where he sat, the paw prints of a cougar were plainly indented in the soft earth. He saw instantly that these were by far the most satisfactory prints he had come across since he had left the pocket far below, so he dismounted and inspected them painstakingly. The clearest impressions, of course, were on the damp lip of the pool, but conditions here were unnatural because of the moisture, and the time element was very difficult to estimate. He came to an opinion, but could hardly believe it. The cougar had paused here to drink within the last couple of hours.

Now, Ki was not one who put much stock in coincidence. Schooled by the wily samurai, with postgraduate work against the Sioux and Arapaho, Ki, on testimony of his compatriots, could cold-track a horsefly across the Big Horns, or name the color of a horse from the shape of its tracks. These tributes were probably exaggerations. But there were certain elementals he had found in years of tracking that he now accepted as truisms.

A horse, for example, would not fly like a bird. Water did not run uphill. And the sun did not set in the east. By the same token, a shrewd predator like this cougar wouldn't conceal its tracks in a rock-bottomed culvert—as had occurred just before Ki had been ambushed—then leave a track like the one around the pool here in errant disregard of danger. Not when it could have paused to drink most anywhere else along the stream and left no track at all.

Ki looked at the trail, which begged to be followed. "That cat's running a barefaced flimflam," he pronounced positively. "But I don't get the hang of it." Ki followed the trail with his eyes to the base of a slope. His gaze lifted. Beyond, the hills rose sharply, and several hundred yards above they parted abruptly as if a giant knife had slashed through them. Serrated rock walls reared to the right and left until they seemed to pierce the sky.

Chuacas Canyon. He didn't know how he knew it was, but there was no question in his mind that up there was Chuacas Canyon. An odd excitement stirred in him as he stared at that gaping fissure in the peaks. There was something grim and evil and forbidding about it that seemed to reach out and clutch at him.

He circled the rock walls from which the stream poured, and had little difficulty trailing the cougar up into the mouth of Chuacas Canyon. Then once more the tracks disappeared. Several hundred yards in width, the canyon floor was clogged with sparse timber and dense, thorny thickets out of which jutted needlelike rock spires and limestone formations that had been carved by wind and rain into the shapes of grotesque monsters. A strong wind swirled through the funnel-like pass, making sounds like sepulchral laughter among the spires and weirdly carved formations. A cloud passing over the afternoon sun threw the canyon into purple shadows.

Ki shivered, feeling the malignant evil of the place, and glanced back the way he had come. He started, hand falling to the weapons in his vest. He was almost certain he had glimpsed a skulking figure back there.

The figure had vanished instantly, like a shadow, into a clump of cedar. It was not in the shape of a cougar, but looked more like the skinny, warped figure of Shukka. Ki shrugged and rode on along the canyon. Likely the old Indian chief had trailed him out of curiosity, to find out what he was up to.

Keeping his horse at a steady jog, Ki followed a worn path through the brush and rocks, stopping now and then to check his course for new sign of the cougar. After riding steadily for almost an hour, he realized the worst was yet to come. The trail dipped abruptly down over a sloping rock shelf and entered a stretch of boulder-jumbled, deeply eroded badlands. Here on the canyon floor, with the late afternoon sunlight blocked by the imposing sides, tracking the cougar seemed more impossible than ever. A thousand dark shadows crawled and twisted over the ground, marking the depths of culverts and crevices where the light did not penetrate. Here and there a smooth granite spire or eroded rock turret jutted above the gloomy surface, looming like headstones in a graveyard.

Giving up all attempt at finding sign, Ki reined in and stared thoughtfully at the way ahead, his senses tuned for any sound or sight that might put him on the cougar's trail again. But all was quiet . . .

Then suddenly the stillness was shattered by the high, thin wail of a cougar. Goading his horse on, he rode swiftly on through the canyon toward the source of the sound. As he did so, a vague uneasiness stirred inside him.

It wasn't until he had passed the patch of badlands and was once again in a stand of trees and tall scrub, however, that he heard another sound— a growling cough to his left. Ki whirled quickly for cover. Drawing his saddle carbine, he slid quietly to the ground and led his horse into the thick shadows cast by a nearby clump of conifers. The sound came nearer as Ki hunkered low behind a screen of bushes and peered tensely ahead.

And up.

And he froze.

Sixty feet above ground, on the thick branch of a tree, perched the cougar. Ki judged that it was a female all right, about a hundred and twenty pounds and a good eight feet in length, including a very long tail. And like all cats, she was extremely graceful and very beautiful with her soft tawny color, free from all markings. She was staring right at him, luminous eyes glowing in the murky dimness, an almost Cheshire-cat grin showing as she bared her fangs in a menacing hiss.

Then, in the next split instant she was gone. She simply leapt into thin air and vanished, it seemed, leaving Ki to wonder if he'd imagined the whole encounter. Hearing the light crack of a twig somewhere ahead, he recovered his senses and moved in swift yet cautious pursuit. The cougar could attack and kill him at any time, he realized, and yet now he was beginning to doubt that this was what she had in mind. For her it was a type of game, he suspected, like cat and mouse—a game that nonetheless was rough and scary, and could turn without warning from play to an uncontrollable urge to test her deadly skills.

Ki had gone less than a hundred yards when he again spied the cougar. She was leaving the far end of the canyon, now just ahead, moving on in a steady, purposeful stalk into covering vegetation beyond the mouth. Ki hastened forward, grasping his carbine. When he was twenty yards from his quarry, the cat again disappeared, suddenly fading from sight after gliding into the shadows of a chokeberry thicket.

Refusing to believe his eyes, Ki headed forward, keeping his gaze on the thicket. Reaching it, he could tell the cat was no longer in the thicket, but he had not heard or seen her leaving it, either. An eerie foreboding ran down his spine as he warily pushed through the thicket, searching for some sign of where the cougar had gone, and sensing he would never find any.

Instead, on the other side of the chokeberry thicket, he came suddenly upon the hacienda. The ruins huddled like the weathered bones of a skeleton in a large circular clearing that was closely hemmed in by the chokeberry, dark timber, and encroaching vines.

The hacienda, Ki could tell, had been built like the castle of some feudal baron. The main building was surrounded by lesser structures—adobe stables, sheds, servants' quarters. At the rear was a small cemetery, and the ruins of what obviously had been a chapel. The entire group of buildings was surrounded by an adobe wall ten feet high. The wall had crumbled in sections; in others it was shrouded by junglelike undergrowth and masses of creeping, coiling vines that writhed like multihued snakes. At the front, sagging iron gates dangled from leaning posts. From these gates a weed-overgrown flagstone drive, flanked by storm-twisted manzanita, led up to the hacienda. The gaunt spires of the two-storied structure jutted toward the shadowed sky like skeletal arms lifted in mute supplication.

Ki shivered again. *"El Rancho de Sambres*—that isn't hard to believe now! I can almost hear the chains clanking around at night."

He was intrigued by the things Eve Rutherford and the sheriff had told about this place. His first conviction that Lester Rutherford had really blundered onto an ancient Aztec treasure trove had been somewhat shaken by Matt Beemis's views, for the Starbuck manager had struck him as intelligent, knowledgeable, and down to earth, a man whose opinions should not be taken lightly. However, Ki was one who liked to weigh the factors and form his own opinions, then act. Treasure or not, he suspected that there was something deadly and sinister afoot here, well worth getting to the bottom of if possible.

"I always hankered to meet a real ghost! Maybe now's my chance, now that that damned cougar's gone like smoke."

Hurrying back to collect his horse, he returned to the hacienda and tied the animal to one of the iron posts, then moved through the gateway and along the weedy drive. He climbed a flight of flagstone steps and crossed a brick-paved patio to great oaken double doors. The doors creaked and groaned as he grasped the rusty handle and shoved, forcing them open. He stepped through into a high-ceilinged room. Huge spiders dangled from webs and scuttled on walls and ceiling. Mammoth rats scurried for holes. A thick layer of dust coated everything.

Ki's eyes narrowed with sudden interest. The imprints of many feet made a bizarre network on the dusty floor. But there were other, larger tracks—boot prints! And moccasin tracks, too, all of recent origin.

He went through into another, smaller room, which, like the first, showed signs of having been richly furnished. Remnants of lovely tapestries dangled from the walls and lay on the dusty floor, along with beautiful paintings. The woodwork was of heavy virgin oak, artistically finished. This second room opened into a wide corridor that extended to the back of the rear mansion, with rooms flanking it on each side. The boot tracks showed clearly in the dust of the hallway and in most of the rooms.

In the center of one of the rooms was a massive trapdoor. It required all of Ki's strength to lift the heavy door by its iron ring. The opening revealed a flight of steps leading downward into musty darkness. Having no light, Ki did not descend the stairs.

But in almost every room, both upstairs and down, he found something of interest. It was a weird, ghostly place, its twisting corridors inhabited by bats, spiders, and rats, and filled with flitting shadows. Once Ki thought he heard the shuffle of feet somewhere in the ruins, and he was certain he heard a door slam. But that was, he decided without conviction, merely the wind.

The sun was almost down when he reluctantly emerged from the ruins. Thick shadows were growing, filling even the higher reaches of Chuacas Canyon. Ki stood for a moment, adjusting his eyes and mind to this sudden change from the musty, ghostly past to reality—then stiffened, alert, as a gunshot crashed some distance away.

Flinging a last glance at the thicket where the cougar had vanished, Ki wheeled and sprinted to his horse. Mounting, he eased back through the timber and undergrowth, wanting to learn who had fired that shot, and why. Yes, and he had to admit he was glad to be quit of the hacienda, too. It had left its mark on him. Evil was there, and danger.

Jumpy, his nerves stretched to wire tautness, Ki rode slowly, eyes wary, hands hovering near his weapons. His horse, as if sensing the need for caution, walked daintily, almost silently. The mammoth music of the wind among the spires and trees was the only sound. Then, although Ki heard no other noise, his gelding lifted its head suddenly to look rightward, its sharp ears pointing. The movement struck a warning chord among its rider's instincts, and he reined in, waiting.

A laugh sounded rightward, startlingly close, low and wicked and brutal.

Ki slid from the saddle and, ground-reining his horse, left his carbine in its boot for stealth's sake and eased through the underbrush. He stopped at the edge of a clearing in the timber that was laced with yellow-belled tornillos and Spanish dagger, and crouched.

On the far side of the clearing, a hundred feet away, Ki could see the figures of three men in the deepening shadows. Two wore grubby, nondescript clothes and boots, and looked ready, in fact downright eager, to kill the third man. This third man Ki recognized as Shukka. The Indian chief was down on his knees, his hands bound behind him, the upper part of his thin body thrust forward, head thrown back as if staring at the sky. Blood ran over his face.

"Talk, you ol' buzzard, or that wet rawhide'll cut your gullet in two!" snarled one of the white men. "Just nod your head when you get ready to cave."

Realization chilled Ki, and a cold rage at the diabolical cruelty of the two renegade whites seared through him. Now he saw that some kind of thong had been tied tightly about Shukka's bony throat and was digging into his withered flesh. It was, he knew from what he had heard, a strip of wet rawhide. As the rawhide dried, it would contract. Shukka, helpless with his hands bound behind him, would be slowly strangled to death—unless he gave the signal that he was ready to tell his captors whatever it was they wished to know.

And the old Indian, Ki reckoned, would die before surrendering. Already his skull-like face was turning black. His eyes, almost bulging from their pits, blazed hate and contempt up at the men.

Something had to be done—and fast. Ki was trying to figure what, when the decision was taken away from him by his horse. Evidently a shift in the wind brought the scent of the other men's horses, for the gelding let out an acknowledging whicker. Ki, having little choice, started running out across the field, forced to count on closing the distance enough to use his knives.

The two renegades whirled, surprised oaths ripping from their lips. Seeing Ki's figure driving headlong at them, they grabbed up their revolvers and began blasting lead. But they had been caught off-balance, thrown into a confusion bordering on panic by Ki charging recklessly at them, and their bullets slashed the air inches from his head.

Then a throwing dagger appeared in his right

hand, and he sent it winging toward the larger of the two men, praying his aim was accurate and he wouldn't hit Shukka by mistake. The man cursed bitterly, spun half about, and fell sideward to his knee. But he came up again, still swearing, and, ripping the dagger out of his thigh, crashed limping into a fringe of timber. Deserted by his wounded compadre, the other man flung his emptied pistol at the leaping Ki, whirled, and dived into the underbrush.

Still furious, Ki started to chase after them. But from the corner of his eye he saw that old Shukka had fallen forward to the ground and lay there twitching weakly, the rawhide thong buried in his scrawny throat. Whirling back, Ki whipped out another knife. The old Indian's tongue protruded, and his eyes seemed ready to pop from their sockets. He seemed to be breathing not at all. Ki thrust a finger under the taut thong, taking no time for gentleness, and slashed through the rawhide.

The Indian dragged breath into his lungs with a rasping sigh. He lay still a moment, gasping, then gradually breathed more calmly. Somewhere off in the thickets, Ki could hear the noisy passage of two horses, the sounds gradually receding. Pursuit was hopeless now. He concentrated on Shukka.

Shukka gazed with expressionless eyes at Ki, rubbing his throat with a clawlike hand. After a moment he rose unsteadily to his feet. "Shukka thanks Squint-eyes for saving his worthless life," he said hoarsely. "The evil ones would have killed me."

"I know. They'd have no doubt killed you even if you'd told them what they wanted to know."

"That I could not do."

"You followed me from the village?"

Shukka nodded. "I was curious about you, Squint-eyes, and sorry I had been forced to order you away from our hogans. The young bucks were angry because you had killed Hopelchén, and perhaps would have done you harm."

"Hopelchén tried to kill me. Why?"

A veil of secrecy seemed to slide over the old chief's pitted eyes, and he shrugged his bony shoulders. "Hopelchén is dead, so no man can ever know what was in his heart and mind. But he was an evil son of an evil father. Perhaps he just had the urge to kill."

"That is not a straight answer," Ki pointed out. "Okay, so what were the two whites who captured you trying to make you tell them?"

"That I cannot tell you either, Squint-eyes."

"The secret jewels of Quetzalcoatl? Was that the reason Hopelchén tried to kill me—because he thought I was after the same thing?"

Shukka's gaunt figure stiffened. All the friendliness left his black eyes, leaving them cold and wary and hostile. "Squint-eyes would be wise to put out of his mind all thoughts of such things," he said stiffly. Then, turning abruptly, he vanished as the cougar had into the darkening timber. His words had been a cold warning.

Ki let him go, even though he felt rankled and frustrated. His eyes were grim and thoughtful as he returned to his horse, mounted, and headed back down to the Anvil range. Still, thinking back over the day's events, he had to admit that he had spent a profitable several hours. Things before only suspected were now certainties in his mind.

Unquestionably, the bloodstained vampire god, Quetzalcoatl, had cast his malignant shadow over this range.

★

Chapter 5

Meantime that afternoon, while Ki was off tracking the cougar, Jessie and Evelyn Rutherford had visited the Forked S, Double Diamond, and Laddered V spreads. Jason Ribeiro, owner of the Forked S, was a crusty old-timer with a vivid vocabulary bordering on profanity, especially when expressing his opinion about the recent rustlings of his cattle. Laddered V owner Neal Limbaugh proved to be a silver-maned and bearded man in his fifties, his august face thoughtful of lip and righteous-eyed; clad in a loose jacket of brown corduroy and canvas pants, he appeared to be what he was, a successful stockman, gracious but somewhat dismissive of women in the ranching business.

The visits with these two men and with Willis Diebold were uneventful, and nothing really concrete came of them. But there was one slight oddity that caught Jessie's eye, which, as she thought it over later, proved rather important.

It occurred when she and Eve arrived at the Double Diamond ranch house. Olin Thayne, the foreman, was on the veranda and gave the two women an impersonal greeting, his lips twisting in a barely disguised leer. In a display of politeness, though, he tipped his hat when Evelyn introduced Jessie.

"Take a load off your feet," he invited. "The boss will be right out."

As they sat down in chairs, Thayne stuck his head in the door and called an order. A moment later there was a sound of boots pounding the floor. Two husky punchers appeared, packing a chair in which was seated Willis Diebold, a blanket resting across his knees. The cowboys placed the chair on the veranda and retired.

Diebold gave Jessie a warm look from his blue eyes. Jessie listened while Evelyn and the Double Diamond owner discussed with Thayne the possibility of a roundup soon. Suddenly her eyes fixed on Diebold's well-polished boots, which rested supinely on the floor, held for an instant, then glanced away. She gazed out over the ranch yard, watching a couple of punchers crossing the storm-muddied ground to the barn, her brows drawing together in concentration.

That was all there was to it. Shortly, with the details of the roundup tentatively agreed upon, Jessie and Evelyn took their departure.

It was late afternoon when Jessie returned to the Twisted Bar. Matt Beemis was just finishing assigning some punchers to new tasks, and greeting Jessie, he remarked that she must be saddle-weary from riding all day.

"No, I've been sitting around talking as much as riding, I think," she replied. "Actually, I wouldn't mind taking a little jaunt over our range, Matt."

Beemis grinned boyishly and suggested, "We'll saddle fresh mounts, then, and take a tour of the south line. I was a kind of mind to, anyhow. We swing through that section regularly,'cause rustlers can strike and get away from there the easiest."

Riding out, Beemis led Jessie on a circuit of the south boundary, wending west to east along a rough, twisty, single-file path. They wound through brush and timber; across gulches and hollows; over corrugated slopes where sage claimed the thin, rocky soil on the high banks, and grass grew lush in pocket meadows where runoff deposited richer soil.

"Keep your eyes peeled," Beemis advised. "Maybe bringing you out thisaway wasn't such a safe idea. Them Quantrell jiggers who steal our beef won't stop at anything, I afear."

After seeing Quantrell's men in action, Jessie figured Beemis was right, and she appreciated his worry. It made her realize and respect the sort of top manager he was, and confirmed her opinion of him as an intelligent, diligent man who was deeply concerned with the welfare of the ranch, as well as of the Malazo Valley in general . . . and it added to her budding sense of personal attraction, a tentative awareness that bordered on sexual arousal. Not that she had any such designs in mind, she hastily thought; it was one thing to admire the man and quite another to desire him.

As they rode, Beemis explained pungently how the Twisted Bar was suffering from Quantrell's gang. Indeed, the Twisted Bar range offered evidence of his words. Jessie could see for herself that livestock was down in number, and though the remaining cows were far from soup culls, they weren't prime, juicy beeves, either, the best having been run off by the night-riding raiders.

81

Presently the trail threaded a series of rimrock slopes, from where they sighted a group of steers some distance ahead. Beemis spurred toward them and yelled, motioning for Jessie to follow, but there were also some other cows bunched yonder in a draw. Jessie called that she'd go flush out this second group, and before the manager could refuse her help, she veered off in their direction.

By the time she was able to chouse the cattle free, the sun was blazing low, burning down the day. Shadows cast long fingers across the range, confusing Jessie for a moment when she glimpsed a flick of movement at the far bend of the draw. Curious, wondering if maybe she'd overlooked a cow down there, Jessie rode to see what she could see. As she neared the corner, a ruffed grouse hen rose, clucking, and ran across in front of her. Jessie grinned to herself—

And riders barged round the blind curve at a floundering canter.

There were three of them, and they were almost onto her. They reined up like maniacs, so close that at first they seemed all enormous horses' chests and heads and bridles, bridle straps and brass buckles, flying streamers of slaver. Then the men loomed behind the horses' ears, dressed like cowhands. Their clothes and saddles had seen a lot of wear and riding. One, spiderlike, was all big chest and little bowlegs. One had the intense, burnished eyes of a lynx. The third was no doubt their leader, for he was the same thick-lipped, hooded-eyed brute who had led the killing raid against Evelyn and the cart driver. All were carrying saddle carbines, not in their rifle boots, but out and slantwise across the inside of their saddle forks, hair triggers ready for a snap shot.

"Looky here," the leader was shouting, aiming at Jessie, "it's that Starbuck bitch!"

There was no space to veer aside, and no time to, anyway. At so slight a distance it would be impossible for them to miss, Jessie knew, and this gunman had all but admitted they would shoot her on sight. She was going down, but she'd try to take at least one with her.

Her fingers went for her gun butt as she kicked free of the saddle.

With a gloating sneer, the gunman squeezed the trigger.

The crack of a big bore gunshot thundered in the narrow way.

Landing, rolling, Jessie came up firing instantly, instinctively, before being conscious of any wound or whether this was her last breath. She missed, but the gunman was no longer seated quite as he had been in the saddle. He was slumping in a lax fall, with half the crown of his head missing.

The spiderlike man was starting to bring his carbine to bear. Jessie shifted slightly and shot him, her slug ripping his throat to shreds as if from an inner explosion. The man's mount went into a small shy, crowding into his partner's mount. This one, the man with the burnished eyes, had his carbine butt almost to his armpit to draw his bead when Jessie blasted him. She shot him twice. Hip-shooting riflemen didn't worry Jessie too much; but bead-drawing riflemen did, sure as hell.

She rose from her crouch, shaken and bewildered. By some inexplicable miracle, she had come through untouched. And the trio had wound up dead, the first stretched faceup under her horse's belly, the spiderlike one curled fetally on the ground, and the last man twisted, sprawling, entangled in his

83

stirrup. Jessie untangled him.

Before she got any more surprises, she reloaded her still-smoking pistol. She then inspected their horses, finding to no surprise that they bore assorted brands from God-knew-where. She was removing the horses' bridles and bits when she heard a rider approaching. She aimed her pistol, preparing to fire.

"Don't shoot!" Matt Beemis yelled, heaving into view. He reined his cow pony to a stiff-legged halt. "That was positively a close one," he said breathlessly. "I had to make a helluva long shot to pop that feller."

"Thanks." Flashing a grateful smile, she holstered her pistol and returned to taking off bridles and bits and hanging them on the horses' saddle horns.

"I saw 'em cross our line and would've plugged 'em then if I'd been closer—Uh-oh, more company coming," Beemis said, peering skyward.

"Your hands?"

"Shouldn't be, not o'er here at this hour."

The only visible indication of the riders was a flock of swallows winging restlessly from distant timber. Staring, Jessie saw another, nearer flock rise disturbed, and she commented, "They're coming, but I don't know if they're after us."

She slapped the gunmen's horses on their rumps, sending them galloping in the direction of the riders. Then, mounting, she started off with Beemis at a spritely trot, heading the opposite way out of the draw. From there they threaded through timber, mostly white-bark pine and hemlock, and crossed an area of shadow, eroded gullies with a million rabbits scampering through dead sage runnels. Beyond this open space they curved in along a creek, joining a game trail that ran upstream along one bank. All this time they had been alert as they rode, but there was no sign of pursuit. Once they reined in, however, and dimly heard riders behind them.

The creekbank trail entered a pass, its floor pretty well brushed over with laurel and juniper trees. The sides of the wide pass were banked rock, pitted and honeycombed for maybe forty feet up, and above these slopes, widening back and up at a slant, seemed to be boulders and juniper. After quite a stretch, the trail curved away from the creekbank due to the roughness of the terrain, and it wove through an interlocking belt of wooded growth and great glazed boulders. Where the trail became crazily serpentine, Beemis slowed and glanced around, muttering that there had to be a path.

There was, cutting away between two gray, chunky stones—unnoticeable unless one knew where to look. Following the path, they crossed the floor and climbed the bank to a ledge, about thirty feet up, in a niche of rock, screened from view by chokeberry and juniper saplings. The rock slope behind it, and above it, was bare and sheer.

Reaching the ledge, they removed their carbines and picketed the horses back by a shallow cave, like a grotto, hollowed in the stone bank. At the rim of the ledge they judged the pros and cons of various spots and crawled into a dense tier of saplings with big, waxy leaves. They lay stretched out full-length on their stomachs, their weapons before them, with a clear view of the trail below.

"This may take a while," Beemis said.

That was fine by Jessie. By now the sun was a molten fireball rimming the horizon, continuing its slow decline into evening, its slanting rays burnishing the western exposure of countryside. The warm, breezeless air and the rays of sunset slanting under their slight canopy of foliage lulled her with an aura of tranquility. She knew they would have to make a stand here if this didn't shake their pursuers—that is, if they hadn't lost them already, and she still had doubts whether they'd been chased. Odds were, she figured, that nobody would come, and she'd get to enjoy some rare peace and quiet.

"This is pleasant, Matt, wherever we are."

"It's a campsite, on occasion, for owlhoots riding for the Malazo Trail," he explained. "It hasn't been used much since we started keeping tabs on it, and after a posse cornered Three-Toed Flanagan here a few years back."

Jessie shifted her body and reflexively Beemis touched her. They lay prone that way for quite a while, aware of each other and stirred by the closeness and the knowing. Jessie could feel his breath against her face and smell the fragrance of his masculine body . . . and gradually, against her will, she sensed stewing tendrils of pleasure beginning to curl in her belly and loins, and she clenched her buttocks in a futile attempt to quell them.

Beemis felt her tensing and touched her again as though he thought she was fearful and needed reassuring. She caught his hand in her own, the gentle caress of her fingers like a magnetic contact . . . and now her face was close, so that there was a blending of warm eyes and ripe lips and clean-scented hair.

"They're green," he mused, gazing into her eyes. He hesitated, self-conscious, but the thrusting impulse to take Jessie in his arms was elemental, without conscious thought or effort. It was as natural as breathing. He just reached and drew her to him and kissed her in the deliberate fashion of a man savoring a cherished delicacy. There was a fleeting moment when the sweet flavor of her lips swept him reeling, beyond regard for who and what she was, the boss lady. Then he released her.

His voice was husky, choking. "An accident. Won't happen again. I apologize. No, by God, it was too delicious for me to be sorry."

Expecting indignation, Beemis saw an obscure amusement soften the contours of her face. Her lips, very red from recent kissing, eased into a slow smile, and she purred, "Then I'm not sorry for it, either." Impishly, she kissed him back on the mouth. "Or for that, Matt."

Provoked by her taunting intimacies, Beemis pushed her down in a strong embrace, feeling her breasts pulsing against him through her blouse. He moved his hands over the material, sensing the warmth of her skin and wishing he could run his fingers across her naked flesh, yet fearing to ask and offend her. They continued kissing with increased fervor, his passion mounting until—

"Naked," he gasped. "I want you naked . . ."

Jessie nodded assent. "You, too."

Beemis fumbled hurriedly to strip off his clothes. Jessie gazed at him, her lips glistening, a smoky glow in her eyes as she shucked bare and stretched out, swollen breasts throbbing, curvaceous hips slackly apart, her tender self exposed invitingly.

Now also nude, Beemis eased alongside her and hovered with both hands prowling over her breasts and nipples. Jessie squirmed, sighing, his touches igniting her . . . and then she shuddered as he dipped his head down to her trembling belly and tongued her navel. She whimpered, tangling her fingers in his hair while his tongue moved farther down and thrust deep, teasing her delicate flesh and tasting her loins. Her thighs clenched spasmodically around his laving tongue and nibbling lips, excitement spiraling up inside her.

Beemis eased his tongue along her cleft, swirling back and forth across her most sensitive area. Jessie sucked in her breath, and exhaled sharply in response to his suckling mouth, spearing tongue, and nipping teeth. A minute . . . two minutes . . . her belly rippled. She began to pant explosively, her hips curving up, her pelvis grinding against his face with pulsating tension . . .

And Jessie climaxed, moaning, twisting in the clutch of her sweet agony. She shivered and relaxed . . . or *tried* to relax, as Beemis continued his darting like summer lightning against her moist pink flesh, and she felt herself building to another crest.

"That . . . that's enough . . . I'm ready . . . Now, now . . ."

Beemis rose and knelt over her. She lay silent with anticipation, her legs spread on either side of him, her exposed center moist and throbbing. He levered downward, and she groaned with the rock-hard feel of him as he began his penetrating entry. She pushed upward, her thighs clasping him, swallowing his full, thick length inside her eager belly, her muscles squeezing around him so tightly that he nearly cried out.

He thrust, then, and she automatically responded in rhythm, mewing deep in her throat, her splayed thighs arching spasmodically against his pumping hips. He licked her cheek and laved her ear. Then their mouths touched, pressing together with lips apart and tongues intertwining. Their tempo increased and increased again to a greedy pace, their naked flesh frantic in their pummeling madness. Beemis's breath rasped in his throat; Jessie's legs cramped where they gripped his middle. There was nothing but exquisite sensation, no existence beyond the boundaries of their bodies.

Then Jessie felt him grow even larger in his pre-orgasmic surge, saw his eyes sparkle with lust, and felt his tension and quickening motions. Beemis's final, bruising thrusts triggered her release again. She moaned, sobbing, as her second climax overwhelmed her, nails raking, limbs jerking violently.

"Ahhh . . . !"

She felt Beemis peak then, felt his juices spewing hot within. She milked all of his flowing passion until, with a last convulsion, she lay still, satiated. Then he sagged, exhausted and drained. They stretched out side by side, their bodies entwined as they gazed out over the ledge for signs of pursuers below and spotted none.

Finally, almost drowsily, she slid free of him and explained demurely, "I have to piddle." Leaving him surveying the view in a contented stupor, she flitted off toward the rear of the ledge, thinking how poorly she'd figured things: Somebody sure did come, okay, and she got to enjoy a rare if not very quiet piece.

But she caught another sound, distant, filtering from down the trail—a faint clicking noise like that made by the beat of horses' irons on pebbly hardpan. She hastened back to the rim, shamelessly nude, her body still hot to the touch as she wedged in beside Beemis. For a long moment there were no more betraying sounds, but when they came—

the jingling of metal against metal—she felt sure
horses were approaching at a goodly pace.

Beemis laid some extra ammunition within easy
reach of his carbine. Jessie loaded her Winchester.
The beat of the irons grew louder, quickly swelling
to a deep, ground-drubbing roll. They lay motionless, sighting on the trail as the first push of riders
careened into view. Behind them streamed more, a
looming flow of big men on big horses, as vicious
and ugly-looking a half dozen as one ever set eyes
on.

Jessie stared grimly, prepared to empty a saddle
or two should any of them chance to see her and
Beemis up here. Luckily the gunmen neglected to
check along the sides. They focused on the way
ahead as they swept around the curves and on up
out of sight, in the direction of the Malazo Trail far
to the southeast.

"We'll have to wait some more," Beemis said, as
the low, drumming pound of their passage was
fading. "Have to be sure they don't stop or double
back."

"Are you hoping it'll be a long, hard time?"

"P'raps. Feel up to it?"

"Do you?" she teased. Then she gasped, "Oh, Lord,
do you!"

His virile manhood was regaining hardness
and girth. Despite being fulfilled and aching,
Jessie found that her loins were responding, pushing upward, clasping his resurgent shaft as he
entered. She closed her eyes, feeling an erotic blaze
rekindling between her thighs . . .

The sunset's last delicate streamers had vanished, replaced by dusk's purple shadows, by
the time Jessie and Matt Beemis got back to

the Twisted Bar ranch house. After a meat-and-potatoes supper, some small talk, and a nightcap glass of brandy, they retired for the night.

Jessie had been given the best of the guest rooms. After lighting the kerosene banquet lamp on the bureau, she sat on the edge of her bed and, sighing, pulled off her boots. The floor was cold to her feet as she padded over to draw the window drapes, then back to where her canvas traveling bag had been placed at the foot of her bed. Opening the bag, she removed her nightwear and wash bag, and then stripped naked, filled the washbasin with water from a matching pitcher, and used a hand towel to scrub herself.

She would have loved a hot bath and a chance to wash her hair, but that would have to wait till morning. Briskly she dried herself with a large towel, her flesh tingling and glowing a healthy pink; then she slipped on her floor-length nightgown. After brushing out her hair and pinning it up, she doused the lamp and climbed into bed.

She lay there, sleepless, thinking.

Finally, with a disgusted exclamation, she got up and went to the window again. This time she parted the drapes and drew up a chair, and sat contemplating for some time, watching the moonlight cast shifting patterns as the branches of a nearby oak swayed gently in a faint breeze. She was still sitting there when Ki returned. She saw him ride in slowly, both his neck and his horse's bent with weariness.

Jessie relighted the lamp and took it with her as she left her room to greet Ki's arrival. Food was the first order of business, and they immediately went to the kitchen, where she rustled up a platter of leftovers for Ki. Then they retired to the little office, shutting the door in order not to disturb the rest of the house, and each proceeded to recount what had been experienced that afternoon and evening—with a certain amount of judicious editing on Jessie's part. The night wore on, and the talk kept on, supplying them with minor details but no more real revelations to share. Finally, with a yawn, Ki rose from his chair and bade Jessie good night.

"I'm too worked up to sleep," Jessie said. She was standing by one of the bookshelves as she spoke, idly perusing the titles, and took down a volume entitled 'Prospecting as a Science.' "I'm not familiar with this text. I think I'll just leaf through it a while, study it a mite."

"By the title," Ki remarked, turning for the door, "I'd say it'd put you to sleep in no time."

Something slipped from between the pages and fluttered to the floor. "What's this?" Jessie asked, picking it up.

"This" was a yellowed sheet of paper covered with figures and symbols. She glanced at it curiously, recognizing it as the solution of a rather complicated equation in higher mathematics beginning "V equals the square root of P plus the cube root of M. ($V = \sqrt{P} + \sqrt[3]{M}$.)"

She handed the paper to Ki, who had paused from leaving. He frowned thoughtfully, the tiny lettering and finely drawn lines striking him as familiar. "Say, Jessie, y'know that strange map the cart driver had? If it's not too much trouble, would you go get it?"

"Sure." Now it was Jessie who left the room, only to return a moment later with the map, taken from her shirt pocket. "You have an idea?"

"Well, maybe." Ki placed the newly found sheet of paper beside the mysterious map. "Isn't the writing identical? It looks to me like whoever worked out this equation also drew the map."

"Why, that'd have to be Zeb Quale!" Jessie stared at the two papers, suddenly noting something that caused her to gasp. "Blazes! What we've assumed for a V on the map isn't a V at all. It's a radical sign! That sentence on the map doesn't read 'V of Malazo to Lazarus—Malazo W.' It reads 'The square root of Malazo to Lazarus—Malazo W,' meaning the square root of the distance from Malazo Peak to Lazarus Mine, I bet. And Malazo W means west from Malazo Peak. I'll bet on that, too. The square root of the distance from Malazo Peak to the Lazarus Mine west of Malazo Peak."

"If that's the case . . ." Ki hesitated, calculating. "I'd estimate the distance from Malazo Peak to the mine as around fifty miles."

"Sounds about right. The square root of fifty is seven, plus. West a little more than seven miles— that would put the point designated well into the mountains over there."

Ki examined the map again, then stabbed it with his forefinger. "Look, Jessie, these lines that don't seem to mean anything. They form a right triangle, with the right angle formed by a line drawn directly south from the Lazarus Mine and a line drawn west from Malazo Peak seven miles, and on that line drawn from the Lazarus, no doubt, near where the angle is formed. That's what ol' Quale was trying to show. This is his map, and the key is in the lettering, although if you hadn't happened on this second paper and seen that he made the radical sign with an unusually short horizontal bar, we'd have kept on thinking the sign was the

93

letter V and getting no place."

"Well, it looks like we're getting someplace now," Jessie said. "And tomorrow morning, we'll go see where this place is."

"I can tell you where it is. At least, approximately," Ki said. "It's just about where I was this afternoon, at the ruins of the hacienda."

Jessie smiled. "Well, now I can sleep . . ."

★

Chapter 6

Gray dawn went into silver dawn, and the silver had burned off in the sky to a medium-deep watery blue, clear and cloudless, when Jessie and Ki reached the edge of the foothills. Climbing, they circled to avoid the Indian village, and passed the spot where the stream boiled from the mountainside, then traversed Chuacas Canyon. By now the sun was near its zenith, glinting in a reflective shimmer off the spires and weird rock formations that lined the canyon floor.

The ruins of Don Fundador's once palatial hacienda huddled motionless and silent in the clear, winy air. In contrast to the funereal wind that had swept through the afternoon before, all lay quiet now, the only noise a scaly armadillo scuttling from the crumbling wall and into the underbrush.

"Even like this, the place gives me the creeps," Jessie said, dismounting. "After dark I imagine it must be akin to a graveyard at midnight on Friday the thirteenth." She flashed a smile at Ki as he climbed down from his horse, adding, "Sayin' is if you don't pester ghosts, they won't pester you."

"Ghosts don't leave tracks," Ki replied grimly. "The Indians are supposed to believe the ruins are haunted and shy away from them, yet there were moccasin tracks in the dust on the floors. And boot tracks." Pushing through the great oaken portals into the high-ceilinged room, he pointed to the dusty floor. "If ghosts did make those boot tracks, they'll also likely pack revolvers."

Jessie slapped disgustedly at a huge hairy spider that, swinging on a strand that dangled from the ceiling, had brushed against her face. She half drew her pistol as a monstrously huge rat scurried between her feet. "Ghosts can have the place for all of me," she grumbled, shuddering. "I can give a good guess what the men who made these prints were looking for—the same thing that men have searched this neck of the woods for for almost a century. The jewels of Quetzalcoatl."

"Then we have to include Zeb Quale in that batch of treasure hunters," Ki said. "After all, we're going by his map. Still, that doesn't explain how the driver got his map, or all the high-grade gold ore in the cart. Anyhow, it's plain that others think there's Aztec loot to be had. Supposedly the idol vanished here in this hacienda."

"Maybe the Aztecs hid it somewhere else before they holed up here. Or maybe not." Jessie rubbed her chin, glancing around thoughtfully. She, like Ki, had seen haciendas such as this in Arizona and Mexico, and knew that many had secret panels and doorways where the Spanish grandees hid their valuables or could hide themselves in emergencies. "Only way to try 'n' find out, I guess, is to go over the place from top to bottom. If nothing turns up— well, all we've wasted is a little time."

Separating to cover more territory and save time, Jessie took the rooms to the right of the long corridor that bisected the old hacienda, Ki those on the left. Jessie examined each room with minute thoroughness, tapping the walls and floors with her gun butt, her keen eyes missing nothing, yet paying scant attention to the lovely tapestries that dangled from the walls, the beautiful paintings that had been slashed and trampled by vandals.

Ki worked just as methodically as he progressed slowly through the dusty, littered rooms. Though he found nothing unusual, his conviction remained that here among these ghostly ruins lay valuable answers if not treasure.

Neither put much stock in tales of hidden bounty. The vast majority were only legends, even though a few—a very rare few—panned out as true. And indeed they knew that a long time ago treasure trains, loaded with bar gold, pigs of silver, loot from wagon trains, even sapphire and pearl necklaces from Mexico's beautiful women, had rolled over the old Malazo Trail. And since this was the stomping grounds for renegade whites and Mexicans and marauding Apaches, many of those pack trains had been attacked. Nobody ever discovered for sure what became of a lot of that treasure, but Jessie and Ki had no doubts that some of it could well remain cached back in hidden caves and caverns. Texas was a big place, an empire within an empire, a country where many strange things could happen . . . and did.

Presently Ki reached the room that contained the trapdoor in the center of the floor. He took hold of the iron ring and lifted the door, revealing, as he had before, a flight of steps that led downward into musty shadows. Leaving the trapdoor open, he headed outside, able to hear Jessie's progress in another portion of the hacienda by the hollow thuds of her boots. Out in the yard, he quickly gathered some fallen pine branches to serve as a torch, then returned to the room, now hearing sounds on the rickety stairs that told him Jessie was ascending to the top floor.

Igniting the pine branches, Ki lowered himself through the opening. The steps were creaky and the makeshift torch sputtered in the musty air that swirled up out of the shadows. Twittering bats brushed like ghostly hands against his face. The silence of a tomb held the place.

At the depth of thirty feet he came to the foot of the steps. He found himself in a big room, the ceiling of which was lined with brick, the walls with huge flat slabs of stone. There were boxes, broken bottles, and shattered wine casks. A number of paintings dangled from the walls. On one wall was the mounted head of a giant wild boar, the rotting skin peeling back from skeletal bones.

Having thrust the torch into a crevice in the floor, Ki made a thorough search there in the musty depths of the hacienda. He went over the floor, over the walls, inch by inch. He knew that others had made this search before him, for their sign was here in the ancient dust. He could hear the silence of the place, feel its resentment at his intrusion, as if hostile eyes were watching him and hating him. After thirty minutes, disappointment lay heavily within him. Apparently this had been Don Fundador's wine cellar and nothing else.

He stared frowningly at the huge boar's head, scarcely seeing it. The thing's exposed tusks snarled at him silently; its shiny eyes glared wicked hate, as it had died glaring hate at those who killed it. Still frowning, Ki went forward and touched the head. It had been riveted in some way to a round protruding knob of rock that seemed a part of the wall. He tested its sturdiness, jiggling it up and down. When it seemed to give a little, he took hold of the thing with both hands and twisted from side to side. The head, and the protuberance to which it was affixed, turned with a squeaky sound.

Then there was a louder, harsher creaking.

Ki leapt backward, then stood very still, staring, amazed. The slab of stone to which the boar's head was affixed was turning slowly, as if on hinges, revealing a doorlike opening in the wall.

The rock slab creaked to a halt. Beyond the head-high opening lay the deep shadows of what appeared to be a rock-walled corridor. In the dark beyond, disturbed bats flitted about in a cloud. Elation surged through Ki—maybe this secret door and hidden tunnel meant something, maybe not, but he was impatient to find out.

Remembering Jessie, he grabbed up the torch and turned toward the stairs, but on impulse he changed his mind and stepped through the opening into the tunnel. Instantly, as if the flat slab of stone he had trod upon were some kind of mechanism, the door creaked shut behind him. Momentarily startled, Ki examined the stone slab from his side. In its center was an iron ring affixed to a protuberance much like the one on the opposite side of the door, and serving the same purpose as the boar's head.

Then, peering ahead, he saw that the tunnel was obviously man-made, several feet wide and high enough for him to stand without stooping. Its walls were lined with rock slabs, its ceiling shored with timbers. That ancient, musty smell was intensified here, and here the same kind of huge hairy spiders crawled over the walls and dangled on webs from the ceiling.

Slowly Ki moved along the tunnel, eyes and ears alert. His footsteps echoed hollowly, and the torch cast flitting, leaping shadows over the walls. Mammoth rats scurried about his feet. A current of damp air brushed like clammy fingers against his face. Then he paused, abruptly, his eyes narrowing with sharp interest as they probed the tunnel floor. Coating dust lay thickly there, and the dust showed unmistakable footprints, many of them. Stooping, Ki examined the imprints. They were moccasin tracks, and were of recent origin. Shukka's followers? Obviously somebody else had discovered the secret door, or there was another entrance farther on someplace.

Tension mounting inside him, Ki went slowly forward again. His spine prickled with the feel of danger, the feel of ancient, hostile spirits staring at him hatefully. But he knew that whatever peril lurked here in this subterranean world belonged not to the musty past but to the immediate present.

At last, rounding a bend in the tunnel, he emerged suddenly into an immense cavern that was like a great, gleaming cathedral. This cavern was not man-made. It was a natural dungeon deep in the earth, as if a giant hand had scooped it out with splayed fingers. Vast white pillars upheld the vaulted roof, and frostlike tapestries, glowing like iridescent fires in the torchlight, draped the walls, Dangling overhead were giant chandeliers of shining stalactites.

For a long moment Ki stood motionless, his eyes photographing the weird place. In the floor of the cavern was a gaping black hole several feet across. To the left of this hole . . . Again that icy tingle raced along Ki's spine, and he stood utterly motionless, staring at the thing—at the golden image of Quetzalcoatl, the crouched, ugly, leering figure of the vampire god!

The idol gleamed dully in the shimmering light of the torch. It was twice the size of an ordinary man, a hulking, paunchy figure crouched atop a stone pedestal four feet high. Its huge hands, reaching out before it, were like a hawk's talons. Its bulbous head was wholly bald, and its broad, cruel features were bisected by a beaklike nose that jutted between predatory eyes. Directly before the idol was a flat, ten-foot-square slab of rock, and at this altarlike slab its eyes were staring with evil and cruelty incarnate.

Ki stepped slowly forward and stood before the sinister figure. A sense of unreality, a feeling that this was a nightmarish dream, enveloped him. But he knew here was the pagan god of an ancient, mysterious race transported to present-day Texas. Steeling himself, he climbed onto the rude altar. And there, once again, he paused, a little shock going through him.

There on the grayish surface of the rock were dark, brownish stains. Not old stains dimmed by time, but vivid, relatively fresh stains—bloodstains!

With a nauseated feeling in the pit of his stomach, Ki recalled the legend of Quetzalcoatl—how on an altar before the image, young and beautiful maidens were sacrificed to appease its wrath. The Aztecs believed that Quetzalcoatl grew angry only when he was hungry, and that his only food was the blood of the victims offered him.

Ki's lips tightened and his dark eyes grew bleak. Wicked things, things more sinister and deadly than he and Jessie had suspected, were entangled in the web of treachery and greed that held this range.

Standing on the altar, he ran his hands over the hard, smooth surface of the idol. Legend also said that the image of Quetzalcoatl was hollow, that inside it was a rich treasure hoard. If that were true, there had to be some way of gaining entrance. Ki slid his fingers over the idol's bulging stomach, shivering at its clammy coldness, up over its thick throat to the gross, leering face. It was logical to suppose that some delicate mechanism, such as controlled the stone door, opened a secret panel somewhere about the idol's anatomy.

Suddenly he heard a low, scraping sound behind him.

He whirled away from the idol, in one hand holding the burning torch, the other stabbing for the weapons in his vest. As he pivoted, he glimpsed two men coming out of the deep shadows at the back of the cavern—Indians. He saw the pistols in their hands, the grimaces of hate on their coppery faces, then saw flame lance from one of their guns. Ducking, still wheeling, he leaped to one side and off the rock altar. He knew exactly where he would land—on the smooth surface of a smaller slab of stone near the gaping hole in the cavern floor. He heard the snarl of the bullet as it whipped past his cheek. He felt his feet land against the slab of rock, felt them slip, and fought to regain his balance.

Then, belatedly, he realized that his feet had not slipped, but his weight had tilted the rock sharply, throwing him forward toward the gaping black hole. He tried desperately to fling himself backward, away from that yawning pit. But the rock slab had tilted too swiftly. His feet slid along the smooth surface, and slamming against the rock with stunning force, he clawed frantically at the stone as he continued sliding toward the hole.

But there was no hold for his fingers. His legs jutted over the edge of the rock into space, then the entire lower portion of his body, and with a bitter despair he realized he could not check his descent. Then he slipped off the rock and fell downward—downward through chill darkness—and somewhere in the inky depths below he thought he heard the sound of running water . . .

Meanwhile Jessie, nearing the end of her part of the search of the old hacienda, opened an upper-story door—and looked into the muzzle of a Remington .44 and the twin bores of a short-barreled brush gun.

Holding them steady on her were two hardcases. The one with the revolver had a little round bald head, as smooth and shiny as a billiard ball, on a big muscle-bound body; the brush-gunner was younger, chinless, without eyebrows, and chewed away at nothing. They both looked to Jessie to be as mean as tarantulas. Maybe not full-fledged professional gunslicks, but that didn't mean they couldn't be hundred-percent butchers. You didn't have to be a slick-draw gunman to be a killer.

"Stand hooked, lady," the brush-gunner snarled.

Shocked into immobility, Jessie stood still, realizing bitterly, that she had walked into a trap. Undoubtedly two of Quantrell's renegades, they had seen her and Ki arrive, and had simply sat still and waited for them. She thought of Ki somewhere on the lower floor, and was thankful that they had separated.

The bald man stepped forward and took her holstered pistol, then shoved her roughly back against a wall. "Whatcha doin' here, bitch?"

"Well," Jessie said demurely, "I was out riding, and I got ever so lost."

The man with the revolver laughed once, derisively. "Balls. Where's your Chink bodyguard?"

Jessie shrugged. Her bluff hadn't worked; as she'd feared, the men had seen them both. "I haven't kept up with him."

"He came here with you," the brush-gunner growled. "We watched you through a window when you rode up. I heard you talkin' down below a little while ago. Where is he?"

"Find him if you want him." Jessie purposely raised her voice in an effort to warn Ki. "You must've been here waiting for us. How'd you know we were coming?"

"We'll ask the questions, bitch," the brush-gunner snapped, and jabbed her with the gun's muzzles. "Marsten, he's somewheres below. Go corral him, but be careful."

"Don't worry, Pierce, I'll get him," Marsten, the man with the revolver said, grinning, and he quietly left the room.

The brush-gunner named Pierce remained with Jessie, eyeballing her, licking his lips like slices of liver. Thumbs hooked behind her belt buckle, Jessie leaned against the wall, trying to seem depressed and defeated, hoping for a chance to draw her derringer. But if Pierce assumed that by taking her pistol they had rendered her defenseless, he kept his brush gun aimed squarely at her brisket anyway. She could not hear any sound from below that would indicate Ki had been jumped by Marsten and taken prisoner. There was, in fact, nothing to hear except a frozen stillness that seemed to stretch on forever.

Eventually Marsten returned to the room, alone. "No sign of him, Pierce. Nothin'. I searched every room, too, even poked into the cellar."

Pierce cursed with disappointment. Leaving Jessie under Marsten's gun, he crossed to a window and peered out. "Both their horses are still here. Huh. Reckon he got spooked and ran away on foot. We'll get him later, easy."

"What about her?"

"Kill her," Pierce replied matter-of-factly, and then he leered. "But not right off, not afore we have ourselves our pleasures."

"Not here," Marsten protested. "I ain't about to have my pleasurin' interrupted by no sneaky Chink catchin' me with my drawers down."

"Good point. We'll take her to the cedar breaks."

Savage rage boiled inside Jessie, along with relief that Ki was still free. Her best bet was to wait, to stall, hoping for an opportunity to make a move, or for Ki to come to her aid, acutely aware that to act now in anger would only result in her being shot down in cold blood.

"Git!" Pierce snapped, prodding her with his brush gun.

Grimly Jessie obeyed, going out the door and down the stairs, followed by the lecherous yet wary outlaws. They tramped along the corridor, out the front door, and over the worn flagstones of the driveway, past her horse and Ki's gelding, which were tethered to the iron railing.

With a last furtive glance around, Jessie walked out past the hacienda, still under gun, the two men right behind her. Following their cursing directions, she headed away from the ruins, toward the mouth of Chuacas Canyon. They did not go into the canyon, but angled along one side, where it funneled out from the mouth and formed a wall of gloomy granite that stretched away for some distance. The bristles of thickets and clumps of stone at the base of the cliff wall were difficult and torturous to negotiate on foot, and formed too shallow and exposed a terrain for the outlaws' evil purpose. Ahead, though, grew some cottonwoods and a cedar break, and it was in there . . .

Trying to find some way to escape, and to keep her mind off what lay ahead if she didn't, Jessie studied the granite wall as she walked. She noticed that after a bit the upper portion of the wall changed. She could see that a lighter colored stone replaced the basic granite that still formed the foundation of the cliff face. The difference in the stone was slight in appearance. It would doubtless have been overlooked by anyone who wasn't schooled in such matters, and who wasn't closely examining her surroundings in desperation. But the line of cleavage, moving diagonally down the wall to the north, was, to Jessie, plainly apparent, albeit useless to her.

Underneath the taller cottonwoods was the dense growth of cedars. Jessie was forced to reach out her hands to break a way through the thicket, the pair behind her in a jocular mood now, obviously anticipating their coming depravities.

"Okay, bitch, far enough," Pierce commanded. "Strip nekkid and let's get to sportin'. Marsten, keep her covered whilst I keep her covered!"

"You!" Marsten snapped. "Why you first?"

Pierce turned to scowl. "I seen her first."

"Well, then, it's my turn to do her first!"

With the two men confronting each other, haggling over the spoils, Jessie had her first—and likely last—split second in which to act. In a frantic lunge, drawing her hidden derringer from behind her belt as she moved, she clenched Pierce's gun wrist with her free hand and swung it outward, at the same time stepping full into him, spreading his armpit farther with the wedge of her shoulder. It was from this position, with her derringer flat against the brush-gunner's side, that she shot Marsten, who was standing a little behind.

It was Marsten who at that instant was the bigger threat. Pierce with his brush-gun might have hesitated before firing at her, aware that the scatter pattern of his load would have blasted Marsten to bloody smithereens as well. But Marsten with his revolver could pinpoint his shot, and he had been doing just that, his trigger finger squeezing, his Remington targeting Jessie. So she had made him her primary target, and nailed him first.

As Pierce tussled with her, Jessie shot him next, up under the rib cage, ramming the stubby barrel of her derringer into the man's clothes as she fired her last shot. He was dead before he hit the ground.

Jessie stood back, trembling. She had killed again. To keep from being raped and murdered, true, and she only had a moment to spare for remorse. There was plenty still needing to be done, and not much time to do it.

And paramount on the list was to find Ki.

★

Chapter 7

To Ki, it seemed that he fell endlessly through chill, Stygian shadows. The rushing passage of air roared in his ears, and he sensed rather than saw or felt the rock walls hemming him in, although once his shoulder struck with numbing force against rock. Inside him was the bitter knowledge that here, barring a miracle, was the death that he had faced and eluded so many times before.

Then he plunged, headfirst, into water that he could not see. As he slashed downward through the icy water, he thrust out his hands to protect his head, and felt them drive jarringly against smooth, slimy rock. He doubled his body, like a fish flipping over, and struck upward. Surfacing, his mind reeled from his fall and his smashing contact with the water. A droning sound was in his ears, and he could feel a strong pull at his body as if from unseen hands. He was in utter darkness. Peering upward, he saw only blackness there, too, and realized that he had dropped his torch when the flat stone tilted. Unless the Indians up there had made a light, the huge cavern would remain in shadow.

He shook his head to clear it, trying to piece together the events of the last few moments. The hidden doorway, the cathedral-like cavern, the nightmarish vampire god staring with malignant eyes down at its bloodstained altar, the two Indians, and the tilting stone that had cast him down into this dark pit. And he couldn't be sure he was not asleep, in the throes of a horrible dream.

He bumped into something, reached out a hand, and clutched a rough edge of rock. His feet found another protruding slab, and he rested there, braced against the tug of current. His shoulder ached with sharp pain. But his head had cleared now, and he knew this was not a dream. He fumbled one-handed for a small waterproof matchbox he carried in his vest, and opened it with his teeth, careful to keep its contents away from the water that trickled down his face. He removed several of the matches, and holding them between his teeth, he replaced the box.

He scratched one of the matches on the rock, holding it above his head. The match sputtered, throwing out a weak, yellow glow over the dripping black walls of a rocky tunnel. The tunnel was perhaps twenty feet wide, and filled from wall to wall with dark, swirling water. The walls, although wet and slimy, were not smooth but saw-toothed, with tiny protruding edges, and they made a curvature overhead, forming a roof which at its highest was no more than five feet above the black water. Beyond the flickering matchlight, in both directions, the underground stream vanished into impenetrable darkness. Above Ki, and slightly behind him, was the funnel-like passage down which he had fallen from the sacrificial cave. There were no steps up to the tunnel, nothing. Even if he could return to the base of the tunnel, it would be impossible to scale the walls to the cavern above.

The match winked out, and Ki clung there to the wet rocks, chilled by the swirling water, cudgeling his brain for some way out of this predicament. But there was no foreseeable way out. He had no way of knowing from whence this stream came or where it went. But one thing was certain. He could not go back the way he came. His salvation, if there was any, lay in following the course of the stream in the dismal hope that some channel of escape would open. His enemies now were not Indians or Quantrell's gang, but this rushing water, the cold blackness and the rock walls of this fantastic subterranean prison.

Releasing his hold on the rocks, he drifted with the current, treading water, keeping within reach of the wall. At times he found he could walk on rock bottom; at others the water was well over his head. Once he was drawn into a fierce whirlpool that spun him around with dizzying speed, then cast him outward with savage violence and against a boulder in placid water. Dazed, breathless, he clung to the wet rock. The water surged against him, tearing at his legs, wrestling him as a human adversary would have.

Grimly Ki scratched another match. In the dim glare the darkness seemed to retreat slowly, sullenly, for a few yards, where it crouched, waiting for the match to go out. The stream, he thought, had narrowed somewhat, the curved roof dropping lower over the water. But there was no turning back. He turned loose of the boulder and drifted with the current again. His feet were on the rocks now, but the current sweemed swifter, its hollow booming filling his ears.

Suddenly he felt something that was like a clubbed fist against his head. He stumbled, ducked his head, and found that it was underwater. He had been easing along with water up to his chin, fighting to remain upright against the current's strong tow. He stopped instantly, some of the water's bleakness seeming to seep through his heart. He fished for anot'ier match and scratched it—and saw that what he had feared was grim reality.

Where he stood, the tunnel roof was no more than a foot above the churning water. Worse still, ten feet away the tunnel narrowed abruptly to a bare half dozen feet, and the roof crowded down, so that the tunnel became a solid wall of churning, leaping, snarling water.

As the match winked out, he huddled there in the ink-black tunnel, thinking with a desperate calm. A thunder like the continuous roll of giant drums beat into his ears. The water swirled about him with a speed much greater than at any other spot, as if hurrying to crowd through the narrowed tunnel. He had no idea how far he had traveled since tumbling into the pit, or in what direction the underground stream had carried him. But now a notion that had been in his mind from the start was crystalizing to certainty.

He lit another match. This subterranean stream, he was fairly sure, was the same one that plunged from the mountainside below Chuacas Canyon. And if that were true, here directly before him was undoubtedly the spot where the water surged forth with its roar of freedom from darkness into sunlight. If he could swim through that water tunnel and let himself be dropped into the pool below, he might have a chance. But even if his assumption were true, he had no way of knowing how far the water-choked tunnel extended before leaping into the open. Ten feet—or a hundred yards? The first meant life, the latter certain death.

But death here was just as certain. He couldn't stay put, and he couldn't go back.

Taking a final look as he held the match aloft, Ki sucked in his breath—and lunged straight toward the spot where water and rock met. Just before reaching the spot, he ducked under. The cold water grabbed him and jerked him forward, pulling him between gaping rock jaws and whirling him over and over in utter darkness. He had no control at all over his movements. He could hear nothing, see nothing, but he knew he was being hurled forward through the narrow tunnel at a terrific speed. He was tossed this way and that, upward, downward, sideward. Several times he was slammed against rock with numbing force.

Seemingly driven relentlessly through a dark, tumultuous night of titanic fury, Ki lost all sense of time and distance. But his lungs had begun to ache and burn and great weights were pressing against his eardrums. He was hurled headfirst against a wall. A purple mist clouded his brain, and a dismal gray certainty of defeat flooded through him.

Then suddenly he felt himself flung outward. Suddenly and amazingly a bright light speared into his eyes. He was falling, with a golden mist of spray engulfing him. He pulled his lungs full of sweet, pure air. And he plummeted down into the clear, placid pool at the base of the walls.

He sank only inches and came up swimming. A moment later he sat on the rocks rimming the pool, bone-weary, but filled with a deep gratitude for his deliverance. Some of his throwing knives were gone. But, miraculously, he was alive.

As he slumped, recouping his flagging energy, he remembered Jessie, and wondered how much time had elapsed since he'd found the secret door and entered the tunnel. An hour? It could have easily been twice that, or only half as much. When he felt somewhat recovered, he got unsteadily to his feet and began plodding toward Chuacas Pass, not looking forward to the long hike through it to the hacienda. He made little effort to avoid detection, walking openly along the center of the trail. If he were attacked now, he doubted he had enough strength left to fight, and he was becoming so numbed with exhaustion that he was almost past the point of caring.

He was to the open patch of badlands when he saw Jessie coming from the other direction, riding her mare and leading Ki's gelding.

"By hell, there you are, Ki!" she called, quickening her pace and reining in beside him. "Where'd you disappear to? You look like you've been swimming with your clothes on!"

Ki grinned wearily. "Where're you going with my horse?"

"Out looking for you before any more of Quantrell's gunnies waylay us," she replied. "A couple of them were in the hacienda and caught me—"

"Hold it," Ki said, swinging into the saddle. "If Quantrell's gang are in this neck of the woods, we'd better get out pronto."

"No, not until I check out something near the hacienda."

Wheeling around, they rode back toward the hacienda, eyes and ears alert. Jessie was disheveled, her face scratched from the thorny thickets through which she had been forced to walk. Ki was

114

hatless, bruised, his clothes water-soaked.

"We make a sorry-looking pair," he said reflectively. "First, suppose you tell me what happened to you, then I'll unload."

Tersely Jessie recounted her capture by Quantrell's outlaws and her subsequent escape. "I don't know if they were waiting on purpose for us or not," she concluded, "but if they were, I'd sure like to find out how they knew to expect us."

Ki shrugged. "Probably they'd been posted there as lookouts against anyone, including Indians. Listen to this!" And in vivid detail he revealed what had happened to him, told of the secret doorway, the leering image of the Aztec god, Quetzalcoatl, the bloodstained altar, the two Indians, his fall into the underground stream, and his fortunate escape. "Now, a few things seem to tie together. First, Quetzalcoatl and the story of the band of adventurers who stole the golden image of the Aztec god from the temple on the shores of Lake Tezcuco is more than a legend. Maybe the idol is filled with treasure, maybe not. The Aztec war party that trailed the adventurers up out of Mexico made their last stand in Don Fundador's hacienda. Before being wiped out they found—or forced Don Fundador to tell about—the secret passage into the underground tunnels, and dragged the idol in there and hid it."

"What about old Shukka and his tribe, and the fresh blood on the altar?"

"There's little doubt, in my mind at least, that Shukka's tribe must be descendants of Aztecs who came up from Lake Tezcuco looking for the idol, and found it. But instead of taking it back to Mexico, they placed it on a pedestal before a rude altar in that secret cave where they found it, and went on

115

with their heathen worship of the vampire god. No
telling how many people have died on that altar!"

Jessie paled. "You can't believe such things!"

"I don't believe in it, but I believe it's happened
and still is happening. That's why the Indians have
tried to keep folks away from Chuacas Canyon.
Quantrell doesn't know about the secret door, but
he suspects ol' Shukka knows where the idol is
hidden, just as he suspected Lester Rutherford had
discovered it. And it appears by the map that Zeb
Quale knew, as well. They're dead, but given time,
Quantrell will uncover the idol, then there'll be a
wipe-out fight between his gang and the Indians."

By now they were at the mouth of the canyon, and
Jessie directed Ki along the granite wall, where earlier she had been forced to walk to the cedar break.
"There may be another reason why Quantrell is
active in this vicinity. And what Quale meant by
his map. That's what I want to check out," she
said, gazing up at the cliff face. She pointed to the
lighter colored stone that had caught her interest
earlier. "Look there. That rock up there is different
from this lower down, although it looks much the
same. It's not an unusual formation. During great
volcanic upheavals of millions of years ago, a strata
overlying the lower granite was thrust upward by
pressure from beneath, or by a lateral squeezing
force. If it keeps slanting down this way, before
we reach the end of the cliff face, it should be low
enough for us to get a good look at it."

After riding for another half a mile, they saw the
the cliff wall ended directly ahead. Almost at their
feet was the sheer drop of a perpendicularly sided
canyon of great depth. The right-angling cliff wall
to the west formed the lofty rimrock of the canyon
west of the point. And here the upper strata of

lighter colored stone had dropped to almost level with the ground.

"Quartz, all right, not granite," Jessie observed, noting the cold, gray surface. "Well, right around here we should hit on what Zeb Quale might've been trying to show, or we won't hit on it at all."

Dismounting, they walked to the lip of the canyon, glancing down into its gloomy depths. Far below they could see shadowy black fangs of stone and the tops of pine trees appearing as fragile as feathers at the bottom of the tremendous drop. They leaned over, craning their necks, and stared up at the western continuation of the great wall. Up and up it soared, beetling surface shimmering wanly in the afternoon sunlight, its crests ringed about with saffron flame.

Suddenly Jessie observed something that quickened her interest. Slanting up the cliff face was what appeared to be a wide ledge that continued until it reached the crest. Pointing it out to Ki, she was at a loss to account for such an unexpected formation. Then the explanation occurred to her.

"That upper rock is softer than the granite," she reasoned. "The granite is like a big cup holding the quartz formation in its bowl. The quartz is the softer stone and erodes easier. Over the centuries, it's weathered more than the granite and has receded from the base rock, that's all. That ledge is the lip of the broader granite base. And it should extend all the way down and around the corner here."

Closer examination proved this to be the case. The ledge curved around the angle and descended until it tapered off to a narrow shelf only a few feet above the ground.

They walked to the beginning of the shelf and peered upward. They could see but a short distance, only to where the ledge curved around a bulge a few yards higher up. They then looked down at the ground and noticed several small fragments of stone lying beneath the shelf. Something in their appearance caught their eye, and Jessie stooped to pick one up. It was cracked and crumbly, and sprinkled through it were irregular lumps of a dull yellow color. Also there were crooked yellowish "wires" crisscrossing the surface of the rock. When Jessie handed it to Ki, he whistled softly as he examined it.

"Exactly the same as the chunk of high grade we took from the salt cart," he exclaimed. "Right here is where that cartload came from! Now to find out where this stuff came from."

Scrambling onto the shelf, they began climbing the ledge. It was narrow at first, but quickly widened. Also, it slanted inward, like the petal of a flower. Soon they found themselves scrambling upward between the towering face of the cliff on their left, and an upward sloping rim of stone on their right. They realized that they would be invisible to anyone who might happen to be on the ground at or near the base of the cliff.

They had covered perhaps a score of yards and were some thirty feet above the ground when they halted abruptly, staring at the face of the cliff. Their attention was fixed on a wide, irregular band of darker gray marbled with black and reddish-yellow splotches that furrowed the cliff parallel to the outer wall of the shelf and extended indefinitely upward. They moved forward a few more paces, and paused again.

Here there was a scooped hollow in the surface of the peculiar-looking band, scored out unmistakably with tools wielded by the hand of man. Chisel and drill marks were plain to see against the face of the rock. And the floor of the shelf was littered with stone fragments.

"Ki, it wasn't the hacienda that Zeb Quale had indicated on his map," Jessie exclaimed. "It was this—the location of a vein of rich high-grade gold ore!"

"Yes . . . And that prospector, Ander! Quale was educated in mining, but not enough of a practical mining man to be quite sure of what he'd found here. So he must've told Ander, or brought Ander up here to show him the ledge and get his opinion."

"But what happened then? Zeb Quale was as honest as the day was long, and he certainly would've told Les or Eve Rutherford of their good fortune. He mustn't have had a chance before the cougar attacked and killed him. Now, if Ander was with Quale when the cougar attacked him, it'd make sense that Ander then stole the map. That would mean—"

"That would mean," Ki cut in excitedly, "that Ander is that salt cart driver. Sure, that much fits. Ander knew, of course, that since the ledge was on Anvil property, he couldn't himself locate the claim. All he could do was sneak out loads of high-grade after he had shaved his whiskers and disguised himself. But how did Quantrell's men catch on to it?"

"Good question. Quantrell certainly must have, because his men shot the cart driver without any warning. And that also explains why they stole the chunk from the Lazarus office and the entire cart

119

from the livery. A careful examination would've shown it wasn't Lazarus ore, and soon as the word got around, everybody in this end of Texas would've been pawing over the whole place trying to locate the ledge. It must've been sheer accident that Quale hit on it, the chances are, although Zeb must've believed there was metal in these hills."

They examined the outcropping with great care, and quickly became convinced it was no mere pocket of rich ore, but a definite vein of unknown extent and doubtless immense value. In an effort to ascertain the extent of the vein, they scrambled up the steep shelf. It wormed and twisted in and out of depressions in the cliff and wound around bulges, so that at no time could they see ahead more than a short distance.

The vein extended for several hundred feet before it finally petered out.

"Plenty of width for easy working, and in depth it may extend for miles down into the earth," Jessie decided at length, and frowned thoughtfully. "And plenty of the pieces to this puzzle are fitting in. Plenty more are still missing. All we've got to do now is get them and put them together, which is liable to be a hellacious job!"

★
Chapter 8

Jessie spent another restless night, mulling over the strange state of affairs plaguing the region. She was no nearer a solution by morning, but did have a few questions she wished to check out, and thought that some additional information might well make a difference—information she could probably garner in a short time from Starbuck headquarters. So after breakfast she and Ki set out for the telegraph office in town.

The sky turned from dawn gray to slate blue, and was budding for a warmer color, when they reached a spearhead-shaped knoll that wedged out from the western hillside into the valley rangeland. The wagon trail wound up and through the knoll, traversing a series of rises and hollows and timbered slopes, before straightening out and wending on northerly toward Hope. They were following the trail through a crop of low willows when both horses shied away from them violently. The coughing snarl of a cougar ran ominously through the morning stillness. Almost unseated, Jessie and Ki righted themselves and stared in the direction of the noise—and saw hovering in a nearby tree the man-eater Ki had tracked the previous day.

Trying to control their boogered mounts, neither rider had a chance to draw a weapon and fire. The cat just crouched there, with almost a light of suppressed mirth in her eyes. Again Ki glimpsed a seemingly bemused and mocking smirk on the hairy mouth as it hissed in warning. And he knew for a certainty that if he or Jessie so much as winked an eye wrong, they would never wink again. There ensued a breathless drag of eternity, in which for Ki there was no time or reality. Only his anger, his rise to a challenge, and the tawny figure of the cat. Then she was gone, leaping into thick underbrush and bounding across the knoll toward the western hills.

"That's it?" Jessie gasped.

"That's her," Ki growled, rankled at the cougar's fearless, almost contemptuous appearance. "Listen, if you're not in too much of a hurry to send your wire, I'd like another crack at bringing that puss to ground."

"Fine by me. Lead on."

Just as before, tracking the cougar started out relatively easy. Sign led them up to the crest of the knoll, then along a precarious route toward the hills. Pretty soon the rangeland fell away, and they clambored up slopes rough with boulders and scrub. Veering northerly along the flank of the hills, the hazardous trail dragged endlessly on, their horses plodding grudgingly forward, needing to be prodded every so often, the scent of the cat heavy and close to them.

Ki kept scrutinizing the terrain for prints or claw marks or the cat herself. Slopes grew steeper and ravines drew closer, and at one point a fast-rippling brook slashed across their path, burbling and stewing, making an S-curve, tall grasses and saplings sprouting in its bend. The trail curved with the brook, and approaching the bend, they glimpsed banks of stone around beyond. They reined in; from here on, the way would be on foot, single file.

Jessie filled her pockets with rifle shells and slid one shell through the loading gate, filling her magazine. Then, wrapping the reins around her saddle horn, she let her horse move at a walk. Because of the frequent sharp bends of the cat track among the boulders, just a few yards apart frequently put Ki out of sight. She found it reassuring when she would see him examining the way ahead, lean and wary, just as she'd glimpsed him last time and the time before and hoped she would the next and the time after that. Occasionally she could hear him checking his restless gelding, the nervously spirited horse having not yet recovered fully from the brush with the cougar.

On they hunted, Ki studying the rimrocks and along canyon walls, then gazing up a ways, gauging each possible point where the cat might lurk to strike. Coming to a fork, he paused and searched for sign. He was now thoroughly familiar with this particular cat's prints, and the stance and probable moves she would make. He found the mark of a freshly indented paw, and started up the right branch of the fork, Jessie tagging not far behind. That was all—one print, yet he couldn't shake a sense of unease, which remained perversely vague, as elusive as the track he was trailing.

Eventually, seemingly hours later, they emerged from a long canyon and viewed sharp pinnacles that reared like waiting fangs beyond. A narrow stretch of flat plateau intervened. They strode on, crossing the level ground in a few minutes and advancing cautiously among the rocks. Here there were no boulders or walls to conceal the cat, and they moved easily up and in between two ridges, then crawled forward through brush to the ridge of a long, curving slope. The slope formed a bank that dropped hundreds of feet to a canyon floor, along which ran a well-rutted wagon trail flanked by brush, with a rugged cliff forming the other wall. The turns were frequent and sharp, the rise very steep.

And at the lip of the rim, the cougar prints vanished.

Ki scoured the ground on all sides and for a number of yards down the slope. Nothing. And the hair began prickling on the nape of his neck. Somewhere nearby, that man-eater cougar had to be stalking the shrouding shadows, but there was simply no sign of where. The cat had disappeared as completely as she had twice the day before. Though he could not keep such disconcerting memories completely stifled, Ki still clung staunchly to practical thoughts. He did not believe in ghosts, and there was no room in his mind for superstition about a devil cat sent by Satan—especially one that had in a very natural manner killed Lester Rutherford and Zeb Quale.

A natural manner . . . ?

A thought began to percolate in Ki's mind, a question to mull over. He had not yet managed to clarify his notion into a full-blown idea, when his faith in logic was reaffirmed. Near the trail below, the cougar parted the thick shrubs and came back into view crossing the wagon trail. And Ki grinned in rueful admiration for the beast.

"If ever a cat earned a right to escape," he remarked to Jessie, "it's that ornery-eyed, smug-faced panther down there. And she would, I expect, if it weren't for us. C'mon."

Hastily remounting, they sent their horses plowing down the bank in hot if reckless pursuit. Reaching the floor, they goaded their snorting mounts through the brush and were just emerging alongside the wagon trail when there came a clicking of hoofbeats and a rumbling sound somewhere to the west. Then a bulky stagecoach, rocking and swaying in its cradle of springs, lurched around a turn and bore down on them.

As they reined aside to let the equipage pass, they noted that two men with ready rifles paced their horses on either side of the coach. They favored Jessie and Ki with hard, searching glances as they passed, but nodded a greeting. Then a turn farther down the trail hid them from view.

"Must be a payroll or gold shipment aboard," Jessie observed, crossing the trail to search for traces of the cougar. "Those guards sure looked ready for trouble."

With a satisfied grunt, Ki pointed out where the cougar had plunged back into the brush. More sign led them westward in a vague parallel run to the trail, more or less midway between the trail and the cliff face, always keeping to the thickest cover. Half an hour later, the tracks curved back toward the trail as if to cross over again. As Jessie and Ki drew nearer, they saw that the trail ahead seemed abruptly to leap off into space. Emerging onto the trail, however, they saw that it made an almost right-angled turn around a bulge in the cliff.

Jessie glanced into the dark depths almost beneath her elbow and shook her head. "Anything taking this bend at faster than a walk, coming downhill, wouldn't stop till it hit the bottom of the canyon in splinters."

Once more the cougar tracks vanished. Ki, doubting that the cat would have doubled back at this point, rode slowly along one side of the trail, Jessie along the other, both of them gazing groundward for fresh sign. For a little over a mile more they rode without any luck. The turns were still frequent, but shallower, easier to negotiate. Not far to the front the crest of a rise stood out with knife-edge sharpness against the skyline. Their horses were toiling up the rise when they were startled by a stutter of shots somewhere beyond the crest.

While they were wondering what they could mean, there was a pounding of hooves and a roaring of wheels, and a ponderous freight wagon drawn by four maddened horses swept over the ridge and thundered down the trail. In fleeting glimpses before they whirled their mounts, they saw that the driver's seat was unoccupied and that over the back of the seat a man's leg, around which the reins were wrapped, stuck stiffly into the air.

For a moment they did not have time to look for more. They were too busy putting some distance between themselves and the juggernaut crashing toward them. But as their horses held their own in the race, Jessie and Ki turned in their saddles and stared back with wondering eyes.

"That man who toppled off the seat may not be dead," Jessie called to Ki. "But he sure will be if that wagon tries to round the hairpin turn down below without slowing!"

126

Ki slowed his gelding, aware he was liable to get squashed against the rock, but willing to take the chance. The wagon quickly gained. As it drew near, he estimated its rate of speed and quickened his horse's gait correspondingly. Soon the tossing heads of the runaway team were level with the gelding's flanks. As Ki had surmised they would, the team shied away from the horse a little. He swung one leg over the saddle and stood in his left stirrup. He let the wagon gain a little more, until the high seat was directly opposite. Holding his mount's speed equal to that of the team, he estimated the distance and leapt.

His clutching hands gripped the iron railing around the seat. He hung for an instant, his feet banging against the spinning front wheel, then with great effort hoisted himself up and clambered into the seat. Swiftly he unwound the reins from about the leg protruding over the back of the seat. From the tail of his eye he saw that the leg belonged to a man who lay on his back on the heaped sacks of something in the wagon bed. The man's face was covered with blood, but he was rolling his head from side to side in returning consciousness. Another man lay on his back, a blue hole between his staring eyes.

Ki shoved the leg out of the way, tightened the reins, and put forth his strength. For minutes his efforts appeared to have not the slightest effect on the racing horses, and the hairpin turn was leaping to meet them with alarming speed. Gradually, however, his perseverance began to tell. The horses floundered a little, their gait became broken. But now the turn was less than two hundred yards distant.

Ki redoubled his effort. His great fear was that the reins might snap under the strain. Then that indeed would be the end. But the heavy leather held. The horses slowed to a jolting trot, a walk. With the turn scarce a score of feet distant, they came to a halt and stood blowing and panting and rolling frightened eyes, but with all the run taken out of them.

Ahead of Ki, Jessie had already reined in and was returning to the wagon. Behind Ki, a voice was calling thickly. He turned and saw the bloody-faced man on his knees, gripping a rifle with trembling hands.

"Look out, feller!" he gasped hoarsely. "Them fuckers are right on top of us!"

Ki leaned over the seat and snatched the rifle from him even as the sound of racing hooves reached his ears. A group of masked men bulged around a turn less than a hundred yards to the rear. Ki did not hesitate; neither did Jessie. The rifle leapt to his shoulder just as Jessie's carbine spat fire and smoke. One of the riders reeled sideward with a yell of pain. The speeding horses were suddenly jerked back on their haunches—but not before Ki's shot struck, the leg of a second man flying from the stirrup. Then came another agonized howl, as Jessie's second bullet hammered home.

A scattering of wild shots answered them. Lead whined past. But sheltered by the high-sided wagon, Ki at the driver's seat and Jessie next to the team offered poor targets. As they lined their sights to refire, a voice bellowed an order. The group wheeled their horses and went galloping back around the turn. Jessie and Ki sent a couple more slugs after them, then lowered their smoking weapons.

The man in the back of the wagon was sitting up on the bulging sacks, looking sick and shakey, but apparently not much the worse for the bullet crease along the side of his head.

"Feller," he said thickly, "ma'am, I'm plumb obliged. I never seen anything that looked as good as you did when you came climbing onto that seat. I was just gettin' my senses back, but I couldn't move or do a thing. I sure figured I was a goner, like poor Jimmy-Joe here. Think them fu— them sidewinders will come back?"

Jessie shook her head as she climbed into the wagon bed and proceeded to bandage the man's wounds with a handkerchief. "I imagine they're still trying to figure out what happened," she responded. "I doubt they'd risk a chance coming back around that bend. They'd expect too hot a reception. The odds are all against them, and they know it."

"What's this all about?" Ki asked. "Since when do outlaws take to drygulching freight wagons around here?"

The man hesitated, then sighed. "Reckon you got a right to know," he said, "and if you'd a hankerin' to grab it off, I figure you've earned it." He gave Jessie and Ki a wan smile. "The Lazarus Mine payroll money is under them sacks—nigh onto twenty thousand dollars in gold."

Jessie stared at him. "We met the stage coming downtrail a little while ago. It was guarded."

The wounded man nodded. "Uh-huh. That was to fool Quantrell. It didn't fool him; nothin' ever fools that skunk. The stage went through without any trouble, but when we come along with the wagon, Quantrell knowed the money was in it, but don't ask me how. Him and his gang throwed down on Jimmy-Joe and me. Plugged us both, but

the horses got scairt at the shootin' and bolted."
He paused a moment, wincing from the pain in
his head, then gestured at the sacks. "This wagon load looks heavy, but ain't. Nothin' but bran
in them sacks. The horses didn't pay it no mind
when they decided to git up and go. Before them
owlhoots could get down off they ridge where they
were holed up—the cliffs end just over the rise—
the team had a head start."

Jessie nodded. "Quantrell no doubt knows every
loose word dropped in a bar, and likely has a few
bribes spread around, too," she said. "Well, we were
on our way into town, and if you like, we'll tag
along. You figure you can drive okay? The sheriff
should be notified and you'll want the doctor to
patch up your head."

"I can take her in," the man said. "I'm the driver.
Poor Jimmy-Joe was supposed to be my leader. The
rifle was hid under the sacks."

"Lucky it was," Ki replied. "Mine is on my horse
over there, and it would have been long for knife
throwing. Lucky, too, those reins tangled about
your leg when you fell. Looks like you sort of got
the best of it." He climbed from the wagon, helped
Jessie down, then said to the driver, "You just take
it nice 'n' easy. Don't worry about the outlaws coming back. I bet they've hightailed and kept sifting
sand."

Despite his assuring words, Ki as well as Jessie
stayed on the alert during the rest of their ride—
not only for the outlaws, but also for the cougar.
But Ki was sure they had lost the cat again, or
rather, she had lost them. Three times in two days,
and what stuck in Ki's craw was that each time the
cougar had disappeared at some important junc-
ture—the ambush, then the hacienda, and now

this attempted holdup. It was almost as though she'd not only been toying with him cat-and-mouse, but in the process had been leading him to specific spots at specific times for specific reasons.

Of course that was nonsense. On the other hand, Ki was aware of legendary accounts from Mexico to Argentina that told of wild pumas helping lost travelers through deserts, or rescuing convicts sentenced to die in the wild. And he had to admit that whether or not these tales and his own experience were imaginary, they created a bond between man and mountain lion, a desire to relate with an animal, which he sought to understand.

They reached the town of Hope without further incident. After delivering the wagon to the Lazarus Mine office, Jessie, Ki, the driver, and the mining superintendent went to the livery to stable the horses, then walked over to report to Sheriff Gillette. Diagonally across from the sheriff's substation was the telegraph office, which was actually a corner portion of the building that housed the stage depot and a freight haulage company. Approaching, Jessie noticed that the Double Diamond buckboard was now parked in front of the telegraph entrance, though there was no sign of Willis Diebold or his foreman.

Sheriff Gillette was morose and irritable, they found, and he swore gloomily upon hearing of the attempted holdup. "Well, reckon I better ride there and look things over," he said, in a questioning tone of voice.

Jessie shook her head. "Don't see as there'd be any sense in it, Sheriff," she answered. "You'd be taking a long ride for nothing. The bandits retreated pronto and took their wounded with them, and they're savvy enough to cover their getaway trail. I figure you wouldn't find anything when you got there."

The superintendent knitted his brows. "Well, I got something here—a driver with a busted noggin. I best get him over to Doc Kunkel. If anything develops, let me know."

The super and the driver left in the direction of Doc Kunkel's office. Jessie and Ki were about to follow, when the sheriff cleared his throat meaningfully, and when the Lazarus Mine men had gone from view, he placed a .45 cartridge and a soiled slip of paper prominently on his desk.

"This was waitin' here when I opened up this morning," he said. "The paper was wrapped around the cartridge and tied with a tiny strip of rawhide, and sometime last night somebody must've rolled it under the door. I reckon it's for you, Ki. Anyhow, I don't know anyone else who's squinty-eyed, no insult intended."

"None taken." Ki unwrapped the paper and frowningly read the few words that had been scrawled on it with a pencil:

I was rude to Squint-Eye who saved my unworthy life. If he will come at midnight to where the sweet water springs from the earth's bosom, I will tell him what he wishes to know.

Shukka

Gillette asked with false mildness, "Care to tell me about it?"

"You mean saving Shukka's life?" Ki replied affably. Shrugging, he briefly recounted the events, beginning with finding the hacienda and ending with his conversation with Shukka. The happenings beforehand, involving the attempt on his

132

life and visiting the village, and the occurrences afterward, including Jessie and their discoveries, he mentioned not at all. As it was, the sheriff listened with keen interest, excitement mounting in his eyes.

"Ki," he declared, "if what you say is true, I've been wrong, stupidly wrong! Apparently, after all, there must be more than mere gossip to this Aztec god business. Shukka is a cunning old buzzard. You never know what he's thinking."

"And tough," Ki added. "He would've died before telling those two cutthroats anything. And then, when he found out I was on the trail of the same thing, he closed up tight as a bear trap."

"We've got to get to the bottom of this, and quickly! Nothing will drive men to such frenzies of passion and evil as the scent of treasure." Gillette slapped a fist into his palm. "This is a chance, though, perhaps *the* chance we need to bust this wide open. It seems that, after all, old Shukka is not ungrateful for your saving his mangy hide."

Jessie made a scoffing noise under her breath. She had crossed to the window with the note and was inspecting it by the light filtering through the dusty glass. She had just happened to notice Willis Diebold exiting the telegraph office, carried by his foreman Olin Thayne, when she heard Sheriff Gillette excitedly exclaim that this was their chance.

"If," she murmured, "Shukka wrote the note."

The sheriff blinked. "What do you mean?"

"Jessie means, Sheriff, that she and I learned a long time ago that things are not always just what they seem," Ki responded. "Not that I have any reason to think Shukka didn't write it. In fact the words of the note sound just like he talked."

"Well, make up your mind! Is it a trick or not?"

"Doesn't matter, really. I've got to take the chance. 'Where the sweet water springs from the earth's bosom . . .' Where would you say that is?"

"Seems obvious," Jessie answered. "Where the stream plunges out of the mountainside below Chuacas Canyon. The stream has meant life itself to the Indians."

Ki nodded. "Well, I better get to riding. I'll leave my horse over to the livery for tending, and rent another mount."

"I'll ride with you," Gillette offered eagerly. "I'm just as anxious as you are to—"

"I'll ride alone," Ki said quietly but firmly. "Shukka might get spooky, and too much is at stake. Thanks just the same."

The sheriff sputtered. "Hold on—"

But Ki, nodding with a smile to Jessie, was already heading out the door.

Gillette made a step as though to follow, but was stopped by Jessie placing a hand on his arm. "By the way," she said. "From what I see, Olin Thayne takes very good care of Mr. Diebold. Did they move here together?"

"Eh? Oh, yeah, they did. Thayne was Diebold's foreman over in Arizona. Diebold owned a spread there. He sold out and came to take over the Double Diamond, which is the biggest and best outfit in the valley, when his dad passed in his chips. Shame about him gettin' crippled up. He always was a big, upstandin' feller. I rec'lect him when he left here. Wasn't but a boy in them days, but was already plenty hefty. Wanted to see the world, he said."

"Did he?"

"Roamed considerable, I gather. Then he sort of settled down in Arizona. Wrote his dad regular. I rec'lect when the word come, a couple of years back, that he'd got shot and crippled. The news plumb broke up ol' Arn Diebold. He wanted Willis to come home then, but Willis decided to head over west. Of course, when his dad took the big jump, he come back to look after the property here, which was likely a heap sight more valuable than his holdin's in Arizona. Why?"

"No reason in particular." Jessie smiled. "A lady's curiosity, I guess. Well, thank you, Sheriff. I best be on my way now."

"S'long. You make sure Ki reports what happens, y'hear?"

Leaving, Jessie crossed the street and entered the telegraph office. The clerk, a turtle-jawed little man, grinned appreciatively at her from under his green eyeshade. She smiled warmly and leaned across the counter.

"Tell me, did Mr. Diebold just send or receive a message?"

"Why, he's sending one, ma'am. I was about to key it through." The clerk held up a piece of yellow notepaper used for messages. "Confidential, though."

"Mercy, I hope so. I'm sending one, too." Favoring him with another smile, Jessie took the pad of yellow message paper from the counter and ripped off the top piece. She folded it and put it in her pocket. On the next piece of paper, then, she composed an innocent-sounding wire to her Circle Star Ranch. The telegrapher was amazed by its expensive length, but would have been even more astounded if he'd been able to read it correctly. Jessie's code was sophisticated and private, known

135

only by herself, Ki, and a few trusted employees of the Starbuck organization.

After paying the telegrapher, Jessie walked to the El Capitan Hotel for a leisurely meal. Both she and her horse were in need a good rest and feed before starting the long ride back to the Twisted Bar.

★

Chapter 9

A thin sliver of a moon was rising in the sky when Ki reached the rocky slopes leading to Chuacas Canyon. Instead of his black gelding, he was riding a hock-scarred splotched paint rented from the livery; at first the paint had proven to be a cantankerous mount, but in the end it had been outperversed by Ki and had given up the notion of throwing him, settling instead for an uneasy truce. Since then their journey had passed uneventfully.

Within Ki, though, anticipation burned bright. It wasn't old Shukka and his tribe who menaced the Malazo Valley; the mysterious Quantrell and his renegades were the ones who in their criminal greed were striking out indiscriminately. But Ki was playing a hunch that Shukka, if he would talk, could go far toward clearing up the situation.

Years along the danger trails had taught Ki the virtues of patience and wariness. But he had also learned that few high-stake games could be won without gambling. If the note left in Sheriff Gillette's office was the bait in a trap set by his and Jessie's enemies, he was willing to take the chance.

Circling to avoid the Indian village, he cut back to the stream. Soon the droning roar of the water surging through the fissure in the wall came to his ears. Cautiously he moved forward, while the droning sound grew steadily louder. In a dense thicket bordering the small clearing that cradled the huge fountain, he dismounted and went forward afoot, pausing at the edge of the clearing. Directly before him, leaping and gleaming like liquid fire in the moonlight, was the column of water that spouted from the mountainside. Timber crept up close to the pool on two sides. Back of the surging water were the purple shadows cast by the cliffs. A transparent gray mist coiled up out of the pool and shrouded the clearing.

It lacked several minutes until midnight. Those several moments Ki crouched utterly motionless in his place of concealment, eyes and ears alert for some sign of movement. But there was no sound except the water, no movement other than the coiling mist.

At exactly midnight, he rose and walked boldly out into the clearing. He advanced without visible sign of suspicion, but every sense was alert, his fingers brushing the weapons in his vest as he approached within ten feet of the surging water, and stopped. Still he had seen no sign of anybody. The mist writhed up from the water and curled about him, seeming to rub clammy hands over his face. While he stood limned in a patch of moonlight, shadows hemmed him on three sides.

Hearing a low sound to his right, he pivoted in that direction. A dim figure detached itself from the shadows and came slowly toward him. The figure, Ki saw, was slight, wore light drill pants and a light shirt, and his long dark hair was uncovered.

138

The man moved silently on moccasined feet.

"Shukka?" Ki called softly.

"It is Shukka, Squint-Eyes," the man said in a guttural voice. "I have come to—"

Ki's hands, hovering near his weapons, stabbed for a *shuriken*. That guttural voice was not Shukka's! It was not an Indian's voice at all, but a white man's. He had walked into a trap!

He saw the figure lunge toward him. At the same instant he heard a hard, swift pound of boots behind him and realized that the real peril lay there. Leaping to one side, whirling in midair, he saw half a dozen gunmen leap out of the shadows and hurtle, toward him. He flung his *shuriken*, and one of the hurtling men crashed to the ground and rolled with a splash into the pool.

Before he could hurl another *shuriken*, the other five drove into him. Seemingly trapped by their swift convergence, Ki had time for only a *kapalabhati* cleansing breath before embracing their attack—*nukishomen-uchi*—drawing them and himself into the circular harmony of the universe.

Ki stunned the nearest man with a back-knuckled "ram's head" jab between the eyes. Without turning, without apparently seeing his target, he stabbed the second with a left-handed thumb and forefinger thrust to the throat, constricting the flow of blood through both jugular veins and dropping the man unconscious. Meanwhile, he stopped the phony Shukka tackling from the rear with a sideways snap-kick; his solar plexus paralyzed, the man sank to his knees, convinced he was dying. But the fourth man managed to come in butting from the other side, knocking Ki just enough off balance so he could gouge his knee in the small of Ki's back and apply a full nelson.

"I got him now! Beat the shit outta him!"

"You betcha!" The fifth man grinned, plunging forward.

Using the man behind him for support, Ki bunched both legs in a flying upward thrust, his heels catching the fifth man square in the balls. The man doubled up, uttering short croaks of agony and confusion.

Then, planting his feet firmly on the ground again, Ki simply backed up. The man behind him, who had both arms and one foot engaged in the lock he had put Ki in, was thrown immediately off balance, and had to remove the knee he'd put in the small of Ki's back, to keep himself from falling. So Ki just relaxed and bent his knees and dropped out from under the full nelson, turning as he did so to deliver an elbow strike just beneath the fellow's breastbone. The man went down, and Ki was just preparing to finish the job with a heel to the groin, when he felt the press of cold steel against his temple.

"You move, and I'll blow your fuckin' pigtail brains out."

Slowly Ki lowered the foot he was planning to stomp with and stood motionless. The man leveling the rifle to his head stepped from the side to the front, and Ki saw he was a little less than medium tall, with eyes like charcoal flecks between greasy folds of skin. His teeth were mossy and rotten-stumped. He moved with his knees bent and his elbows out, as though he had just lighted from a jump, or was just getting ready to jump. He was an ugly-looking mortal to Ki, and a deadly-looking one. Ki's face became taut, expressionless, as the

140

rifle continued to bore into his temple.

The five fallen men began stirring, crawling and gasping raggedly, then tottering upright, holding themselves, hacking and wheezing.

"S'mbitch," the one who'd been hit in the balls croaked. He was still in a crouch, one hand cupped over his groin. "You nailed the bastard, Yeager. C'mon, let's pay him back!"

The men all staggered forward, lunging at Ki. They were big, husky, range-toughened brawlers, used to absorbing a lot of punishment and dishing it back out. Yet it was likely none of them would have been alive, much less standing, if Ki hadn't been caught by the rifleman named Yeager. But he had been caught, so the men were standing, crowding in, while Yeager held Ki at bay with his finger tight around the trigger.

The infuriated men surged forward, bent on revenge, arms seizing and fists smashing. Ki stumbled, blinding pain seeming to shatter his skull. He was pulled to the ground, dragged, and kicked.

"Hey, don't kill him!" Yeager cautioned. "Not yet!"

Ki gritted his teeth against the brutal impact of boots. He fought his way to his feet again, using fists, elbows, teeth, knees, his entire body, as a weapon. But it was useless. Despite his spirit, his defiant will, Ki was only human. Blackness overcame him, and he slumped, unconscious, to the ground.

His senses returned gradually, as numbed impressions:

The bent-over hunch of his body . . .

Jarring pain in his wrists, ankles, and belly . . .

The sight of moonlit ground moving past him at the pace of a horse's walk, and the sound of a complaining voice in back of him . . .

One other thing Ki knew: he was alive.

He finally became aware of the fact he was tied hand and foot, and that he was jackknifed over the saddle of his paint. Craning his head about, he caught sight of four gunmen, two in front and the other two behind him, and of Yeager riding point, mounted on a close-coupled grulla.

"Dunno why the boss picked me to go," a rider in back was whining. "My guts're all busted up inside from that kick, I just know they are, and this jouncin' hurts like pissin' hell."

"Shut up bellerin' like a sick calf," Yeager retorted harshly. "You ain't half as bad off as Mike or Lonnie are, and Fletch here, he can't talk much above a squeak after his throat got squozed."

The riders lapsed into silence, emerging out onto a thin strip of a pass between the mountains and the foothills. They were high, Ki realized, and climbing higher, on a wandering, little-used trail no better than an animal track. More than that he couldn't tell.

Ki closed his eyes and slumped his head, and quietly tested the ropes binding him. They were tight and well knotted—but not tight or knotted enough. A slight, humorless smile creased his mouth as he twisted and flexed his wrists and ankles, sensing the weak points, and then relaxed, feeling more confident, and began rebuilding his vital psychic strength. Calming his mind, he focused his concentration on an internal point just below his navel, the place the Chinese call *tan t'ien*. As he adjusted his breathing he continued pressuring the ropes lightly with his wrists and ankles, but he made no overt move to break loose; he was more concerned

142

with restoring his essential energy, and was willing to wait, playing the prisoner, to learn why he was alive. It was no accident; there must be a reason he hadn't been killed . . .

For all its meandering, the trail kept generally climbing. In single file, the riders crossed a winding bench, passed a cloaking forest of tall brush and timber, and were almost through a patch of thick chaparral when Yeager turned his horse directly toward the wall of growth that flanked the trail on the left. The growth extended up the slope of a spur in an apparently solid bristle.

Yeager rode straight for the fringe of chaparral, forced his horse into it, and was swallowed from sight as the next rider entered behind him. Ki had no choice but to follow on his paint. A crackling and a swaying, and he was through what was really but a thin straggle of growth, although a man riding within a yard of it would not have spotted the fact. Ahead stretched a narrow lane cut through the chaparral for a distance of perhaps twenty yards, ending in a dark opening in the swelling rise of the slope.

In line with the other riders, Ki rode through the opening into what he supposed was a cave, the irons of the horses clicking on the stony ground. The line halted at Yeager's grunted order. Yeager dismounted and went deeper into the cavern beyond, leading his horse. A light flared in the darkness. Yeager reappeared, holding aloft a lighted lantern.

"Let him loose," he ordered.

The man who'd tried to pose as Shukka drew a hunting knife and sliced the rope that held Ki down across the saddle. Ki dropped like a feed sack to the ground, landing on his side. His skull still throbbed, and his brains felt as if they were scrambled from the knockout he had suffered. He lay still, breathing through his mouth, as he felt the man cut the ropes around his ankles. Then he was hauled to his feet and shoved forward, causing him to stumble slightly as he began walking into the cavern. He used the opportunity to glance around, and he realized that the cavern was manmade, the tunnel of an old mine. Behind him he could hear his other captors scuffing along in his wake, the irons of their led horses ringing on the rock floor.

For perhaps fifty yards the tunnel burrowed into the mountain. Then abruptly it widened into a room hewn in the stone, a room some thirty feet in width. Ahead, about the same distance, Ki could make out the continuation of the narrower tunnel.

"Hold it," Yeager growled. He placed the lantern on a rough board table, struck a match, and proceeded to light several lamps bracketed into the stone walls. Ki gazed about with interest at the outlaw gang's hideout.

The room had been roughly fitted up as living quarters. Several bunks were built along the walls. There were some homemade chairs, a Dutch oven, a number of cooking utensils, some coarse crockery, and a supply of staple provisions on a shelf. Over to one side was a hitch rack capable of accommodating a dozen horses. To this rack the gunmen tethered their mounts and the paint. Then they turned their attention to Ki.

Yeager's eyes gleamed hotly as he stepped up to Ki, muttering under his breath. "Well, reckon you don't feel so pert as you did when you downed my bunky," he snarled, and slapped Ki across the face, hard, with his open hand. "Okay, boys, search him."

They searched him with relish. Discovering his daggers and *shuriken*, they stripped him of his vest, and almost of his pants when they found his *tanto* knife. They even took his *shurushin* rope belt, although they weren't quite sure if that was a weapon or not. They continued their search, turning him virtually inside out, and he felt fortunate not to have been left naked. Finally they stepped back with baffled remarks.

"He ain't got it," Yeager growled. "But he knows where it is, like as not with that floozy Starbuck he sides, you can bet on that."

"I'll make him talk," growled the man Ki had jabbed in the throat. "I'd sure like to have the chance. I'm in favor of cashing him in right now. It's the safest thing to do."

"Maybe so," Yeager admitted, "but orders is orders. Herd him back into the hole and we'll fasten him up."

Ki was pushed forward again, past his heap of belongings on the table and into the rest of the tunnel, Yeager bearing the lantern behind him. For some sixty paces the tunnel ran straight with unbroken walls; then an opening yawned on the left. Into this Ki was forced. Yeager held the lantern high, and Ki's breath caught in his throat.

The room, about ten feet square, had evidently been used as a storehouse of sorts. Rusty picks and shovels and bars of curious design were scattered about. And some six feet out from the far wall was a row of thick iron rods set into the rock about three feet apart. The row continued around the far end wall also, Ki noted. To these uprights were secured stout chains riveted to the iron. The chains ended in ponderous manacles, and nearly all of the iron cuffs were locked about what had once been a human wrist, but now was fleshless bone.

Some of the pitiful victims lay prone; some were hunched over with knees drawn up to their bony chins. In most cases the corpses had dried and desiccated in the hot, dry air, until instead of skeletons, they had become grotesque mummies with parchment skin drawn tight over the bones beneath, eyeless sockets staring, shriveled lips drawn back from teeth in grotesque grins. From some of the skulls still hung lank black hair.

The black hair, the darkness of the skin, and the prominence of the cheekbones identified the dead to Ki. They had been Indians, doubtless the slaves held captive by the old Spaniards and forced to work the mine. Here they were kept locked up at night. For some reason they had been abandoned by their heartless captors to die a slow and torturous death by thirst and starvation. Doubtless a hundred years, and perhaps much more, had passed since they had sat down to their last long sleep in the dark.

Yeager held the lantern high and gave an evil chuckle. "You'll have company while you're waitin' for the boss. And I reckon these other bastards will have company while *they're* waiting for Judgment Day. Come over here!"

While the other men stood alert and watchful, Yeager picked up one of the clanking manacles that showed signs of recent oiling and use, clamped it around Ki's wrist, and locked it with a key he took from his pocket.

"You ain't the first gent this's been used on," he remarked, gesturing to a corner where something lay huddled. "Over there is another bastard what

146

got in the boss's way—or what's left of him. He'd already been plugged, but you look purty husky. Reckon you'll be able to last quite a spell, even though you're liable to wish you couldn't. A feller gets thirsty mighty fast in here." He chuckled again, malevolently, then turned to the other men. "Fletch, you're stayin' here at the hangout while we go meet the boss. C'mon, boys, he'll be waitin' over to the forks to find out if we dropped a noose on this bastard before he decides whether to come over here or ride on south."

They trooped out together, taking the lantern with them. Ki sat down in the dark, his chain clanking unpleasantly, and mulled things over. It wasn't hard to guess what they'd been after—that map he'd taken off the salt cart driver. Most likely they'd been looking for it when they'd ransacked the mine office, figuring if he and Jessie left the ore with the superintendent, they'd have left the map with him, too. Now they knew *he* didn't have it, and would probably torture him to talk, and when that didn't work, use him as bait to lure Jessie up there to her certain death. If he didn't work out something in a hurry, it'd be all over when the boss, whoever he was, got there. And Ki had a notion that would be soon.

Blindly he examined his manacle with his fingers. The iron cuff fitted snugly about his wrist, and the chain, while rusty, was evidently firm enough. A tentative tug or two convinced him it was far beyond his strength to break it. It was securely riveted to the upright bar, and the bar was set deep in the stone of floor and ceiling. He could hear Fletch banging about in the other room, and soon the smell of frying bacon and boiling coffee drifted into his prison. After a while Fletch quieted down, save for an occasional rattle of knife and fork. Then silence ensued.

Ki listened intently, hoping the silence meant Fletch had fallen asleep. Impatient as he was, he decided to wait a little longer, for he was almost certain to make some noise. If Fletch heard, he might get suspicious and investigate. Slowly the minutes dragged past, and the silence continued. Ki could stand it no longer and began freeing his wrist from the manacle.

Focusing all his concentration on the task, he purposely dislocated the bones of his wrist, then his hand, even his nimble fingers. Then, by merely twisting and stretching his ligaments and muscles, he slowly wormed his limp, formless flesh through the wrist iron, cradling the iron with his other hand to keep it from dropping with a clank to the floor.

He stood, snapping his bones back in place, and groped about cautiously for the scattering of picks and shovels and iron bars. Locating a stout bar, he picked it up and stole silently out of the chamber and along the tunnel. He reached the outer room and peered cautiously into its lighter interior.

Fletch sat at the table, his back to the inner tunnel mouth, his chin sunk on his breast. He was undoubtedly drowsing. Ki stole out of the tunnel and entered the chamber, the bar gripped and ready. He raised it aloft.

And like a feral animal sensing danger, Fletch woke up. He leaped to his feet and whirled about, a hand streaking for his revolver. Ki leapt forward and struck. The blow missed Fletch's arm, but it struck his drawn revolver squarely, sending it spinning across the room. Ki whirled the bar for a second blow.

148

Fletch dived under the swing with more swiftness than Ki would have credited him for. The bar whizzed harmlessly over his head, and Ki's wrist crashed into Fletch's shoulder. The force of the contact opened his fingers, the bar clanged to the floor, and before he could recover, Fletch's huge reaching hands fastened on his throat in a viselike grip. Backward and forward the two men reeled in a silent death grapple.

Fletch, though nearly a foot shorter than Ki, was many pounds heavier, and he seemed to be made of steel wires. Ki chopped at his head and neck with the callused sides of his hands, but Fletch buried his face against Ki's chest and grimly held on. Ki tore at the man's corded wrists but could not loosen the terrible grasp of his thick fingers. His lungs were bursting for want of air; his head was spinning. There seemed to be a red-hot iron band tightening and tightening about his chest. Before his bulging eyes a thin, opal-tinted mist formed. And still Fletch tightened his awful grip.

With the strength of desperation, Ki hurled himself backward. He struck the stone floor with a bone-wracking crash. At the same time he jerked down on Fletch's wrists with every ounce of force in him, driving his leg, stiff as an iron rod, upward. The throttling fingers tore free from his throat. Fletch's body shot into the air. He howled in pain as he turned a complete somersault and hurtled downward, landing on his head, his body stretched out at an angle. There was the thud of Fletch's skull on the stone, a sharp crack, then an odd spasmodic tattoo of boot heels pounding the rock floor.

Ki staggered to his feet, gulping in great drafts of air. Reeling and swaying, he stared at Fletch, who lay on his stomach, his head twisted about at a horrid angle, so that his distorted face glared with fixed eyes over his right shoulder.

"Busted his neck when he landed!" Ki muttered between gasps for air, leaning against the stone wall. For minutes he sagged there until his brain cleared a little and his strength began to return. Finally he straightened, stood rocking on his feet a moment, then staggered to the table to collect his vest and weapons.

Somebody had removed his horse's rig, which lay nearby. Ki cinched with trembling fingers, located his saddle carbine, and slid it into the saddle boot. The urgent necessity now was to get away before Yeager and the other men returned with their boss. Weak and shaken as he was, Ki knew he was in no shape for a desperate battle against overwhelming odds. He paused only long enough to take Fletch's revolver and turn out his pockets. He discovered nothing of any significance. Sticking the revolver behind his belt, he led his horse out of the tunnel into the night air. Getting into the saddle was a considerable chore, the cantankerous paint making it as difficult as possible.

With only the slim crescent providing moonlight, the brush-flanked lane was black as pitch, but Ki sent his mount along it at a good pace. Without slacking speed, the paint crashed through the thin fringe of growth—and then Ki reined in sharply.

Several riders were streaming up the trail, with Yeager at their head. Spotting Ki, drawing revolvers, they spurred recklessly toward him—all except one, Ki saw, who halted at the edge of the chaparral, then whirled his mount and rode back out of sight. He could hear this unseen man yelling order to the others.

"Cut him off! Don't let him get away!"

A gun blasted and a bullet snarled wickedly past Ki's head. But Ki was already in motion again, jabbing his heels into the paint's flanks and lashing with his reins. Bolting into a long, stretching gallop, the paint raced straight for the oncoming riders. Amazement, then alarm, struck at the men's faces as they saw the crazy-eyed paint and its rider slamming headlong at them. They swerved, scattering.

Only Yeager tried to hold his ground. He snarled an oath, and lead-fanged fire spouted from his gun muzzle. Ki felt the burn of the bullet along his left side. Then Yeager, suddenly realizing his peril, tried to whirl his grulla and get away. But he was too late. The paint, running full speed, hooves churning the earth, hit Yeager's horse with incredible force. The grulla was knocked from its feet. Yeager hit the ground and rolled, hoarsely yelling his terror. The paint reared and slashed downward with its front hooves at that screaming, scuttling figure. There was a hollow-sounding crunch, like a melon being smacked with a mallet, and the figure stopped screaming and scuttling.

The paint stormed on into the mass of riders, and now Ki began firing Fletch's revolver. Howls split the air. The paint struck another horse shoulder to shoulder and sent it sprawling to the ground. Ki's flailing gun barrel crunched against bone. Then they were through the whirling, demoralized tangle and flashing along the trail. Guns boomed behind them, lead whined past as the men tried to regroup. Ki, bent low in the saddle, twisted about and blazed lead back at the milling outlaws. One of them slumped forward, then tumbled to the ground. The riderless horse shied away, throwing the mounts of the others into still greater confusion.

151

Just before Ki drove into the timber, he again glimpsed that shadowy figure who had halted at the edge of the chaparral. Who was that rider, and why had he remained back out of sight?

Ki thought he had the answer. This rider who had been reluctant to show himself, even when it appeared that Ki was hopelessly cornered and doomed, had to be the so-called Quantrell, the real leader of the outlaw pack.

Stifling a reckless impulse to circle through the chaparral and attempt the capture of the bandit chief, Ki kept on his way. For he knew that this would be suicidal. The gunmen were rallying, and weapons roaring, they were driving at the spot where Ki had vanished into the forest.

Some of the unaimed bullets came perilously close to Ki. Thorny branches slapped at his face and ripped at his clothes. He crossed a spiny ridge, and the gunfire died away behind him. Sighing with relief, but still keeping every sense on alert, he angled down through the foothills toward the valley, a frown of puzzlement furrowing his brow as he remembered the rider who had lurked back in the chaparral. Who was he? That question was still tormenting him when hours later he rode into the Twisted Bar ranch yard.

★

Chapter 10

Ki slept in late and took his time about rising, every muscle, tendon, and ligament of his body feeling the effects of the night before. He felt better after a meal and a workout, though, and then closeted himself with Jessie to discuss what had happened.

They were still considering what course of action to take, when Sheriff Gillette arrived from town. "Got a wire for you," he told Jessie upon greeting. "Gabe, the telegrapher, swore it was the longest message he ever took."

"Thank you." Jessie opened the envelope and began reading the encoded message from Starbuck headquarters.

The sheriff turned to Ki. "Now, spill. Did you see Shukka?"

"No, it was a trap. Quantrell's men caught me and took me to their hideout. Or what *was* their hideout; Quantrell's too shrewd to keep them holed up there now, knowing I'll be telling you about this." And Ki went ahead to explain the events, until Jessie interrupted to show him the telegram.

153

"Sheriff, you might be interested in this, too," she told Gillette. "The message confirms what you told me yesterday about Willis Diebold and Olin Thayne, and that Diebold was indeed paralyzed by a bullet that lodged in his spine. The doctors were afraid to remove it and gave Diebold less than a year to live. After his father died, Diebold sold his Arizona ranch to come here, and set off with Thayne and another puncher named Alex Niles. Diebold was well thought of and liked in Arizona. Thayne has worked several years for him and had a reputation as a top hand, and though he was rumored to have run cows in from Mexico, no charges were ever brought. My informants can't find anything on Niles, other than that he originally hailed from Texas and worked for Diebold for only a few months."

"Well," Gillette grunted, "that don't tell us much we didn't already know."

Ki, however, sat staring straight ahead of him, his eyes brooding. At last he said, "Sheriff, mind taking a paseo to the Quantrell hideout?"

"Sure! Think you can find it again?"

"Given time . . ."

It took time. Heading northwest from the Twisted Bar with Jessie and the sheriff, Ki rode into the hills swiftly yet cautiously, watching for Quantrell's gun crew as well as for familiar landmarks. He had a keen sense of direction, and felt he was generally following the route he'd taken to escape, but then the terrain had been shrouded by night, and now it was reversed for him. Keeping on his mental trail was one long headache.

A half dozen times, Ki had to rein in to carefully study the deceiving perspectives. Twice he found

154

he'd strayed off course, and had to backtrack, listening to Gillette swearing under his breath. And once he got lost and wound up in a box canyon, then overshot his return, passing the point where he should have resumed his unmarked way. When he realized this and was about to swing back again, he recognized the forest that bordered the thick chaparral that hid the mine tunnel.

Finally reaching the stretch of screening brush, Ki led the way through the fringe. They halted and listened. All was quiet, however, other than the moan of the wind through the growth. The mine tunnel was silent and deserted. Inside, Ki struck a match and lighted a lantern they had brought with them. The outer rock-walled room was much as he had left it the night before, except that the body of Fletch was not in evidence.

"I figured they'd be sure to take Fletch with them," Ki commented. "I hope they didn't think to take the other one when they cleaned out, and I've a hunch they didn't. It would hardly be recognizable by now, anyway."

"What other one?" the puzzled sheriff demanded. "What're you talking about?"

But without replying, Ki led the way to the inner chamber where he had been shackled prisoner. Both Gillette and Jessie exclaimed at the mummified corpses of the Indians, but Ki did not waste a glance on them. He hurried directly to the corner where lay what looked to be a bundle of rags, but which was the shrunken, desiccated body of the man Yeager boasted had worn the prison chain prior to Ki, the man who had "got in the boss's way." Nearly all the flesh had sloughed away from the dead man's skull, but the skin of the body remained stretched over the bony skeleton.

Ki stripped off the rotting rag that had been a shirt, to bare the shrunken chest. Below the ribs on the left side showed the scar of an old bullet wound. He turned the body over on its face. No corresponding scar showed at the back.

"This won't be pretty," he warned, drawing one of his knives. "But it's necessary." With swift, sure strokes he made incisions in the parchmentlike skin on either side of the spinal column. He cut away sections of the skin and the withered flesh and removed several ribs. Suddenly he uttered a sharp exclamation. "See it? Stuck in the backbone?"

"A bullet," Jessie gasped.

"Uh-huh," the sheriff gulped. "Sure as shootin'."

"And just as I expected," Ki said. "A slug lodged in the spine, the bullet the doctors were afraid to remove, and which paralyzed Willis Diebold."

"This's Diebold?" the sheriff blurted. "Why—Why then, that'd make the Diebold over at the Double Diamond a cussed imposter, and a cold-blooded killer to boot!"

"Exactly!" Jessie exclaimed. "Of course, it makes sense! The man posing as Willis Diebold, the cripple, must be Alex Niles, the cowhand who left Arizona with Diebold and Thayne."

Sheriff Gillette leapt erect. "C'mon!" he barked. "We'll put the arm on the coyote pronto. Folks o'er Arizona will recognize him as Niles, not Diebold, right off."

"Whoa up," Jessie cautioned. "We haven't much on him and Thayne—yet. You could have him sent to prison for fraud, and that's about all. In a mighty short time he would be out and causing trouble again."

"But he cashed in poor Willis Diebold! Here's the body!"

"To prove he's dead, that's all. There's nothing to show that Diebold didn't die of natural causes. Remember what my message said, Sheriff—that the doctors gave Diebold less than a year to live. Niles and Thayne would swear the trip over here was too much for him and he died before he got here, and that then they cooked up the scheme to gain his inheritance. No, we're not ready to move just yet."

"How're we going to get the goods on 'em, then?"

"I don't know yet," Jessie admitted. "Let's go. We've got a long ride back to the ranch. Maybe we'll think of something by then."

Sheriff Gillette continued to swear and mutter as they got their horses ready. "And that thievin' murderer fooled everybody in the valley!"

"No reason he shouldn't," Ki responded. "The set-up was perfect. Diebold left here nearly twenty years ago, when he was little more than a boy. Niles must have his general build and looks. Somebody might still have noted differences in appearance, but the chief thing was—everyone was expecting a cripple. That was fixed in every mind. A cripple showed up, so naturally no one doubted he was Diebold."

"Moreover," Jessie added, "Olin Thayne was with Diebold a good long time, in Arizona, and likely knows all about Diebold's early life, and he came here with a pretty good idea as to who lives here and where. Also, Niles originally hailed from Texas, maybe from around this region, which would make it still easier for them to carry on the deception. All set? Let's hit the trail."

It was past nightfall when they arrived back at the Twisted Bar.

157

Matt Beemis was in from his day on the range and was relieved to see them. "Stay for supper, Sheriff," he invited. "Fact is, you might want to think of spending the night. It's getting ready to rain cats and dogs, or I'm a heap mistook."

Beemis proved a good weather prophet, for by the time supper was over, the rain was coming down hard and the night was black as the inside of a bull in fly time. Sheriff Gillette, however, buttoned on his slicker and insisted he'd best ride on to town. Beemis sent one of the hands to ready the sheriff's horse, and he and Jessie and Ki were on the porch bidding Gillette a safe journey, when suddenly someone raced into the yard on horseback. Lightning crackled and writhed across the heavens, and in its sullen red light the horse and rider were etched clearly.

"Somethin's wrong!" Beemis snapped, and ran into the yard, followed by the others.

The rider came on toward them. He was bent low in the saddle, quirting the horse, which was running at a reeling, crow-hoppy gait.

"That's Scat Vanion, Eve Rutherford's foreman!" Beemis cried out, and ran in front of the horse, waving his arms.

The horse came to a slithering halt, its hooves geysering up mud. The rider drew himself partially erect in the saddle and peered at them, swaying a little.

Leaping forward, Ki helped Beemis take hold of the blocky rider and ease him down, then carry him out of the rain, to the porch. He felt something wet and sticky on the rider's shoulder and knew that Vanion was wounded. He could hear Vanion's quick, ragged breathing.

"Steady," Gillette murmured. "What's wrong?"

"S-sheriff? I tried for town to git you, but... found I couldn't make it, had to stop off here for help."

"Dammit, Scat!" Beemis blurted. "What happened?"

"That ravine that comes out of the timber and runs past the barn," the foreman mumbled. "The hellions sneaked up the ravine and hit us—Slim, old Limpy, and me—before we knew what was happenin'. We put up what fight we could, which wasn't much. Slim and Limpy are dead, and they must've figured I was too, for they left me layin' in the dust before the bunkhouse. When I came to—"

"Eve! What about Eve?" Beemis cut in. "Was she there?"

"Miz Evelyn was gettin' preserves from the shed out back. Last I remember half a dozen of them snakes has hold of her and she was fightin' 'em. When I come to, they were gone and so was Miz Evelyn. I reckon they took her away."

"Curse Quantrell's black soul! When I—"

"Wait, Matt, don't go off half-cocked," Jessie cautioned. Then she asked Vanion, "Were they Quantrell's bunch, or who?"

"Indians! Some of Shukka's tribe. I recognized some of 'em."

"They say anything before the attack?"

"Not a word. Just started shootin'."

"We're wastin' time!" Beemis raged. "We'll burn their hogans and wipe the swine out! We'll need a posse!"

"I know how you feel," Jessie said. "There may not be time for a posse. I think I know what the Indians are up to. They're Aztecs, remember, not Apaches." She turned to Gillette. "Sheriff, ride to

159

town, pronto. Send the doctor out for Scat here, and then get a posse together, as big a one as you can and as quick as you can, and head for the old Don Fundador hacienda at Chuacas Canyon. You know where that is?"

"I sure as tunket do."

"When you get there, come down into the wine cellar. By that time you'll know what to do."

"Gotcha!" Gillette rushed for his horse, while Jessie, Ki, and Beemis carried Vanion inside to a guest room.

"Git outta here, git goin'" Vanion groaned. "I'll hold t'gether fine till Doc Kunkel gets here. Wish I could ride with you. Miz Evelyn—I done all I could."

"What now?" Beemis asked Jessie as they left the room. "We ride for the old ruins, like you're havin' the posse do? What makes you think the Injuns will take Eve there?"

"Because that's where the vampire god, Quetzalcoatl, is!"

For a moment Beemis failed to grasp the significance of this. Then he showed a bitter, desperate face and raced out toward the horse corral. In the red glow from a lightning flash, his rugged features seemed carved from stone, his eyes showed like slivers of green ice.

Shortly, wearing slickers, astride fresh mounts and loaded with arms and extra ammunition, the three galloped out of the ranch yard. This night, Jessie sensed, would bring the showdown. It would bring victory or final defeat—and the odds were a hundred to one against victory. Eve Rutherford was in no less danger because she was in the hands of Shukka's band instead of Quantrell's cutthroats. And the fact that the Indians were not lawless criminals, measured by white man's standards, made not the slightest difference. Shukka and his followers were more Aztec than Apache, and could have but one reason for abducting Eve Rutherford. Jessie chilled to the marrow as she thought of that reason. She knew Aztec lore and custom.

As they rode fast for the western hills, the wind slammed and mauled them, and rain came with it in driving, blinding sheets. The cloud masses boiled almost above them. Lightning blazed its red challenge out of these masses, and thunder crashed and bellowed. Driven by desperate urgency, they crossed the black plain, slogging through mud and fording gullies that had become full to their banks with surging, muddy water. And upon reaching the base of the timbered foothills, they pushed on without pause, the rain driving at them like a million tiny spears. They came to the stream, to the spot where it surged from the earth's bosom— and Chuacas Canyon lay before them.

Without hesitation they rode into its gaping, grinning mouth. Here, funneling through the pass, the wind hit them with renewed force. It crashed among the trees and howled a dirge among the rock spires. Between lightning flashes, they were forced to feel and fight their way through the boulders and dense thickets. Thunder boomed and rocketed among the cathedral-like formations. When lightning writhed across the sullen sky, the spires and walls were shrouded in a weird glare. Chuacas Canyon, caught in this mighty battle of the elements, seethed and trembled and bellowed, a violent place of lurid red flames and evil-filled shadows.

Ki suddenly yelled something at Jessie and Beemis, and pointed. There before them lay the old ruins, like the rotting bones of a skeleton

161

in the rain and eerie light. Leaving their horses tethered in a nearby thicket, they paused at the edge of the clearing, and when lightning blazed, they studied the scene before them carefully. There was no sign of movement or life about the hacienda ruins. Crimson serpents of lightning twisted in and out of the gaping windows and over the pillars.

"Come on—come on!" Beemis urged, his face haggard and drawn with worry.

"Easy," Jessie warned. "A wrong move might ruin everything."

"Follow me." Ki led the way swiftly and without stealth now, across the flagstones of the driveway and through the great oaken portals. Not even the giant rats were astir now. The ruins were as still as a grave. Flickering lightning glow jumped through the windows to play over the walls.

By this weird light Ki took them into the next room and along the corridor to the room where the trapdoor opened down to the wine cellar. The trapdoor was closed. Still there was no sound except the screaming wind, the patter of the rain, the rough trampling of the thunder across the tormented sky.

Ki lifted the trapdoor, and they descended the steps into the cellar. The lightning did not penetrate to here, and the only light was a match in Jessie's hand. The cellar was as Ki had first seen it, with the secret panel closed.

"There's nobody here," Beemis groaned. "Looks like we guessed wrong."

"Too soon to tell that," Ki replied, and took hold of the snarling boar's head on the wall. There was a creaking, grating noise as he twisted the head slowly but firmly, and the wall panel slid slowly open.

Jessie had dropped the match, plunging the cellar into darkness. She now stood in utter black, hearing the grating sound and realizing that the panel now stood open, but she could see nothing. Nor could Matt Beemis, who drew in his breath sharply with disappointment. Then Ki lit a match of his own, revealing the open panel.

Ki stepped through, followed by Jessie and Beemis. The panel creaked shut behind them. Extinguishing the match, he whispered, "No more light, no more noise from here on."

Slowly they padded along the dank, musty tunnel, feeling their way. Rats scampered about their feet. The darkness seemed an evil, cloying substance crowding in upon them. Presently a dim, wavering glow of light showed ahead.

"We're approaching the cave," Ki whispered. "At one side of the entrance is a line of boulders. We'll try to get behind them and take a gander at what's happening."

Again they started easing forward. The light grew steadily stronger, and now they could hear voices—a wordless, chanting sound. Moments later they crouched behind the line of waist-high boulders lining one wall at the entrance to the sacrificial cave, and peering over them, they stared, aghast, at the weird, barbaric scene before them.

Eerily, the huge cavern was lighted by the flickering glow from a dozen torches thrust into crevices. The light gleamed on the vast white pillars, and raced like flowing blood over the frostlike tapestries that draped the walls. It glowed dully on the crouched, malignant figure of Quetzalcoatl, the vampire god, whose talonlike hands were outstretched with predatory eagerness toward the rude altar before it.

A chanting, singsong sound filled the cavern, coming from the throats of perhaps two score men who huddled cross-legged in a semicircle about the golden idol. Their faces and bodies, naked from the waist up, were daubed and streaked with paint. They swayed slowly in time with the chant. These, clearly, were followers of Shukka. The old tribal leader himself sat slightly to the fore of the others, his skeletal face distorted by some pagan passion, his skinny body swaying with a ghastly rhythm.

In the space between the worshipers and the altar danced the giant figure of an Indian who, naked and painted like the others, wore a hoodlike affair over his head. This, obviously a wolf skin with the snarling head left on, also was hideously smeared with paint. Clutched in one hand as he writhed and chanted and swayed, this hooded figure held a long-bladed knife.

Stretched on the altar, naked to the bone, bound hand and foot, her eyes wide with terror, was Evelyn Rutherford.

Jessie heard Beemis's low, bitter curse of fury, heard a boot scrape against rock. She quickly placed a restraining hand on her impetuous manager's shoulder. "Wait! They haven't hurt her yet, but they will if you go barging in on them."

Beemis groaned with helpless anger, but sank back and gradually relaxed.

The guttering torches cast weird shadows over the sacrificial cave, causing the paint streaks on the bodies of the swaying figures to writhe like snakes. The rhythmic chant was like the sound of a wind out of dark places, holding something wild and pagan and ancient. It fell to a low moan of anguish, then rose to a shrill cadence of utter triumph and ecstasy. The gibberish that spewed from the hooded figure became louder, his gyrations growing faster and wilder as he leapt and whirled and danced.

Jessie watched, wary and grim. It wasn't hard to figure that Shukka and his followers thought that Quetzalcoatl was angry at something they had done, and they were pleading for his forgiveness. Did they believe the cause of anger was that Lester Rutherford had in some way discovered the hidden panel and entered this cave, thereby violating the presence of their sacred god? And did they hope to assuage Quezalcoatl's wrath by delivering to him as sacrifice the daughter of the man who had committed that outrage? Jessie tensed with apprehension.

Suddenly the wolf-headed Indian stopped his mad gyrations and stood a moment, poised ready to spring. The chanting gradually quieted, the swaying ceased, and the painted figures sat entirely motionless, an expression of unholy expectancy on their gargoylish faces. Abruptly the hooded man leapt, knife upraised, straight at the bound girl. Eve Rutherford's horrified scream rang through the cavern.

Again Matt Beemis snarled a furious curse; he reared up from behind the boulders, gun in hand.

And again Jessie grasped his wrist, forcing the gun muzzle upward. "Hold it!" she admonished. "That medicine man doesn't aim to kill Eve with that knife. Believe me, he'll only draw a few drops of blood from her, not enough to hurt. Watch!"

Reluctantly Beemis subsided.

As Jessie had predicted, the hooded Indian checked his deadly lunge just short of the ashen-faced girl. He stood over her for a moment, the wolf skin a snarling mask, then bent slowly forward. A vast hush lay over the cavern now. Old Shukka and his followers huddled, utterly motionless, without sound, watching the scene before them as if the world's fate depended on its outcome. Six inches from Eve's throat, the blade dropped suddenly. Eve flinched, but did not cry out. The hooded man jumped back, and a murmur rose among the surrounding worshipers.

Staining Eve's throat was a tiny trickle of blood. The worshipers of Quetzalcoatl swayed forward a single time, their foreheads touching the floor. Then they got quickly to their feet, wheeled, and stalked without order toward the cave's outlet. They passed within feet of Jessie, Ki, and Beemis, silently staring straight ahead, and went on along the tunnel toward the secret doorway. Their footsteps gradually receded, and light from the single torch among them, carried by the hooded medicine man, grew dimmer and dimmer and finally vanished.

When the hidden trio were certain that the Indians had really departed, they leapt from behind the boulders and rushed across to the girl on the altar. Ki drew one of his knives and hastily cut her bonds, and with Beemis, he assisted Eve to her feet. Shuddering, she turned her eyes away from the crouched, leering figure of Quetzalcoatl in whose shadow she had lain. With a bandanna Beemis wiped the thin stain of blood from her throat. Beemis covered her with his coat.

"It didn't hurt," she said tremulously. "I didn't even feel it. But I—I thought I was as good as dead."

"Jessie, I owe you," Beemis declared. "If you hadn't stopped me, I'd have done something that'd got us all butchered."

"Forget it," Jessie said quietly. "Ki and I have seen almost the same ceremony down in Mexico, so I knew what to expect. Otherwise I'd have been shooting it up with you."

"That awful thing!" Eve was looking again at the bloated idol on the pedestal. "Is it really Quetzalcoatl?"

Nodding, Jessie explained, "Yes, and for centuries the sacrificial ritual has been carried out as it was here, just now. The worshipers draw a few drops of blood from the victim's throat, then go away and don't come back for a long time. When they do return and find the sacrifice dead—starved, of course—they believe their vampire god has drawn all the blood from its body and killed it. As with these torches, a light is always left burning in the sacrificial chamber to furnish light for Quetzalcoatl's feast."

Eve shivered again, and Beemis placed a big arm about her.

"The idol's supposed to be hollow," Ki said, and stepped without reverence across the altar and onto the edge of the rock pedestal where the idol crouched. Along its columnar legs, over its protruding stomach, through its splayed, clawlike fingers, he pressed, felt, tugged. The metallic statue was cold and smooth to his touch. He ran his hands over the bald, bulbous skull, pushed on the bulging eyeballs, twisted on the beaklike nose.

There was a grating sound and Eve exclaimed, "Look!"

A foot-square panel had slid open in the center of the idol's broad chest.

"Hand me up a torch, Matt," Ki said, and paused as Beemis lifted one of the burning fagots and gave it to him. Holding it close to the opening in the idol's chest, he looked in, then reached a long arm down inside, and they heard a jangling sound. Then Ki withdrew his arm and stepped down to the altar. Grinning, he asked, "Okay, who wants to take a look?"

They all did. Ki held the torch up so that its light sifted through the opening.

"Jumpin' blue blazes!" Beemis exclaimed. "So it wasn't a pack of lies. Gold and silver bars!"

"And jewels!" Eve gasped. "They glow like fire in the light."

"Aztec jewels." Jessie nodded. "Precious stones. One piece of the stuff would be worth a small fortune in New York, London, or Paris. The jewels of Quetzalcoatl!"

"And they're mine!" a voice cried out triumphantly.

All four whirled toward the cave entrance.

Men were streaming from the tunnel, guns in hand. At their head was the phony Willis Diebold, Alex Niles, followed closely by Olin Thayne. Behind these two crowded a dozen other shadowy figures.

And they all had murder on their minds.

★

Chapter 11

Realizing that they faced instant death at the hands
of Niles and his men, Ki leapt backward, his arms
sweeping with him Jessie and Eve. Matt Beemis
was an instant behind, equally desperate to gain the
shelter of the idol before screaming lead cut them
all down. They hit the hard earth with stunning,
bruising force. But they were still alive—for the
moment—behind the crouched idol and the broad
pedestal on which it crouched.

"Get 'em, you idjits—kill 'em!" Niles was yelling.

Jessie and Beemis snaked their pistols over the
edge of the pedestal, and their snarling thunder
slammed over the cavern. Two of the men howled
and fell sideward to the earth. One remained there,
and the other scuttled like an immense spider for
the shelter of the boulders at the cave entrance.
Others sought the same shelter from the defenders'
bullets, while the remainder dived behind other
boulders and jutting slabs of rock lining the cavern
wall. Niles kept yelling at them, from some place of
safety, cursing them, urging them to attack.

The cavern seemed to explode in a red holocaust of gunfire and howling lead, as the barricaded gunmen blasted wildly at the idol. The four defenders flattened themselves against the cave floor, hearing the wicked hiss of bullets as they caromed off the pedestal and the figure of Quetzalcoatl. Fragments of stone showered over them. Grimly Jessie tried to gauge their chances—and saw none at all. At least a dozen and a half men were arrayed against them. To such a fight there could be but one ending. Quetzalcoatl, after all, would have his victims, his blood!

After an initial flurry, the gunfire slackened, becoming scattered shots drumming from among the boulders and rock slabs. But there was a murmuring among the gunmen, too, under the lash of Niles's cursing tongue, a growling and a stirring. A bottle was passed from hand to hand until it was emptied, then another started the rounds.

Jessie thought with dismay of the posse she had told Sheriff Gillette to recruit. How much time had elapsed since their arrival here? It seemed like ages, but she knew that in reality it had been less than half an hour. It would take time for the sheriff to reach Hope and gather a big posse. Then possibly the riders would pause long enough to get a few drinks inside them. And they wouldn't cover the ground between town and the ruins near so quickly as had she, Ki, and Beemis. No, they hadn't had time, not nearly. And they wouldn't have time.

The stirrings were louder among the rocks lining the cavern walls now. The murmurings among the gunmen had risen to taunts and yells flung jeeringly across the cave to the four behind the pedestal.

The torches flickered and guttered, casting a reddish pall like fresh blood over the scene.

"There's only four of 'em!" Niles was bellowing. "Only four—and two of 'em are wimmin—between you and half the gold in Texas!"

"Say your prayers!" a harsh voice called, and almost a score of men surged up from behind the boulders like a black wave of death, the torchlight shining on their drawn guns and their greedy faces. Flame lanced from gun muzzles.

Jessie's pistol blazed as she fired deliberately. Matt Beemis crouched shoulder to shoulder with her, while Evelyn, weaponless, could only huddle in mortal fear. Ki straightened, making himself an inviting target as he tossed daggers with efficient dispatch. Gunmen dropped, drilled by lead or punctured by knives, some screaming and writhing, others ending their misspent lives without so much as a whimper. More men charged on, goaded by Niles's raging voice.

But halfway across the cavern that yelling, shooting wave of death faltered, broke, halted. For a lithe form, its naked body painted from the waist up, had leaped from the tunnel into the cavern, followed by another, and another. Shrill yells rang out from these figures, and shots. And other forms crowded in.

Alex Niles had not led the charge of his men, but now, in the face of this new menace, he came plunging out of the boulders. His face was twisted into a satanic mask of baffled fury.

"It's the Injuns!" Olin Thayne bawled. "Fight your way outta here or they'll massacre us to the last man!"

The gunmen whirled back toward the cave outlet.

But Shukka's yelling, enraged horde met them head-on. They came together in a confused melee of gunfire and slashing knives. The roar and fury of savage, no-quarter battle filled the cavern.

Jessie, Ki, and Matt Beemis leapt out from behind their barricade. Ki speared a gunman in the base of his neck, the dagger passing between the vertebrae and slicing his spinal cord. Jessie shot another gunman smack in the face, the man's startled shout dying stillborn. A third man had his mouth open wide to yell, too, but could not because a bullet from Beemis's revolver had severed his windpipe, along with his jugular veins, which fountained blood as he toppled over.

As though holding Jessie responsible for this turn of events, Alex Niles drove at her, his face snarling with hate, a long-bladed knife in his hand. Seeing Niles almost too late, Jessie writhed away, crashing with force against the idol. She felt the knife blade slash through her shirtfront, heard Niles grunt with vicious triumph, and smelled the unclean scent of the man in her nostrils. With the cavern reeling before her eyes, Jessie rolled away, clubbing at Niles with her gun barrel. Niles stumbled backward, but braced himself, saying something that Jessie couldn't make out above the din of battle.

From the corner of her eye, then, Jessie saw another man break away from the knot of fighting, swearing men, and drive at her. It was Olin Thayne, and Thayne had a gun in his hand. Jessie had a second of indecision, with peril on her right and peril in front of her. Which should it be? Moments seemed interminable, with the death battle between Shukka's followers and the gunmen unfolding before her eyes. Knives flashed and guns roared and smoke fogged thick. The cave floor seemed littered with bodies.

Then Jessie's decision was made as Thayne leveled his revolver to fire. And Jessie shot him, and shot him again, and dodged as Thayne charged headlong into the crouched idol. Thayne rolled away from that leering figure, crashed to the cave floor, and lay still, either dead or mortally wounded.

By then Niles was leaping for Jessie, the rage of being kept from a fortune he had thought was his turning him wild. Jessie twisted away from that savage blow. As Niles surged past her, Ki suddenly appeared, reaching out and seizing Niles by the belt and collar. His great muscles bunched, he lifted the squirming Niles high above his head and threw him away violently.

Niles landed almost in a sitting position on the flat stone beside the yawning hole in the cavern floor. The stone tilted, sharply and quickly, as it had with Ki the day before. Niles screamed, showing a white face stained by terror, as he slid along the stone toward the yawning pit. Fingers and boots clawed frantically at the smooth surface.

Ki leapt forward. But he was too late. Alex Niles slid over the edge and plummeted downward into the blackness and cold and death that lay below. For Niles, even if he were not killed in the fall, would never have the courage or strength to accomplish what Ki had accomplished.

Ki jerked his gaze away from the pit. The battle still raged full fury, although it had taken a deadly toll. The gunmen had put up a desperate fight. A score of Indians were on the cave floor, and old Shukka stood nearby, outside the circle of fighting men, his wrinkle-embedded eyes alight with a fanatic flame. Ki stepped over to Shukka, making no threatening gesture. The ancient Indian stood his ground, watching Ki warily.

"Shukka," Ki said curtly. "When I give the signal, call to your men to stop fighting."

Shukka shook his head. "You white devils must die. By violating the temple of our sacred god, you bring this fate upon yourselves. Shukka has spoken, Squint-Eyes."

"Then Shukka will speak again." Ki's voice was flat, deadly calm. "A posse is due here anytime, and if they find you have killed us in cold blood, they will raid your village, kill you and all your men, leave your widows and orphans homeless."

Shukka said nothing, but the flame dimmed in his old eyes. Reluctantly he called out to his followers in his own tongue. Even as he spoke, Ki cupped his hands to his mouth and shouted, "Okay, break it up! The fight's over!"

The commands had a magic effect. White man and red broke apart, and the fighting stopped instantly. The few remaining gunmen hesitated, looking from Ki to their own dead. All the defiance went out of them, and their weapons thudded to the earth. Matt Beemis, smoking revolver in hand, began herding the cowed gunmen to one side.

"Shukka," Ki said, "tell your men to drop whatever they're holding."

"My men are guilty of no wrongdoing," Shukka said stubbornly. "They were but protecting what belonged to them. They fought because you white devils violated the sacred presence of our god. Is there wickedness in that?"

"Maybe not," Ki admitted, then pointed to Eve Rutherford, who now stood beside Beemis. "But that girl was kidnapped and brought here against her will."

"It is so." Shukka bowed his head. "It is a law of our race that cannot be broken. If the great Quetzalcoatl becomes angry, he who has incurred that wrath must be brought forward and offered as sacrifice so that the god's vengeance may be lifted from our people. Or, if that man is dead, his nearest of kin. It is the law."

"No harm came to her, so that can slide for the time being," Ki said. "But two of her ranchhands were killed when she was taken, and that's a crime in any man's language."

Again Shukka bowed his head, and his body seemed to shrink even smaller. "That, too, is so, and I am sorry. I ordered that there was to be no bloodshed. But those who went for the girl were young and hot-blooded. They hate the whites, and perhaps there was evil in their hearts. They disobeyed my orders, and killed."

"The sheriff will want to have them."

"The sheriff cannot. They are dead, all of them."

Ki's eyes narrowed with thought. He had no way of knowing whether the old Indian told the truth or not. Nor did Jessie, who had come over and was listening to the conversation. Now she spoke up:

"It's not for us or the sheriff to decide innocence or guilt here, Shukka. Somebody else will decide that. The sheriff will have to take you where it can be decided, though."

"But our beloved god, the precious things he holds inside his sacred belly!" There was entreaty in the old Indian's words and tone. "Surely these things do not belong to the white man to desecrate and destroy!"

"No, they don't," Jessie said promptly. "That's one thing I think I can promise you. Your idol, and everything in it, will be sent back where it came from, turned over to the descendants of the people it was stolen from a hundred years ago. Texas will be glad to be rid of it! Texas thieves stole it, and honest Texans will give it back."

Shukka nodded. "I believe you."

"Then tell your men to drop their weapons!"

Shukka spoke a single word, and the Indians instantly let whatever weapons they held fall to the floor.

As Matt Beemis and Eve Rutherford began collecting the weapons of red and white man alike, Jessie and Ki walked over to the man she had shot, Olin Thayne. Alex Niles was gone, and most of his gunmen were dead. Only four survived, two of them wounded. It was something of a surprise to find Thayne still alive, barely, lying on the ground, breathing in hoarse gasps. A quick examination told Jessie he was mortally wounded and going fast.

"Thayne?" Jessie said. "Thayne, tell me something."

Thayne's lips quirked slightly in a ghost of a smile. "Ask it fast."

"Your boss, Alex Niles, was the so-called Quantrell, right?"

"Yeah . . . But in a sense we all were. We'd take turns acting the part, so's to confuse witnesses trying to describe Quantrell."

"And you had to wear masks, so you wouldn't be identified as Double Diamond crewmen, right?"

Thayne nodded. "Niles eased out most of the old Double Diamond waddies and replaced them with our men, but we still got to be known by face around the valley as workin' for him. Had to be careful."

"Still, it was a simple enough scheme for running an outlaw gang, under the circumstances. Easy to get by with, with nobody having any reason to suspect anything off-color about the Double Diamond setup." Jessie hesitated, gazing at Thayne's contorted face. "Burt Ander, the prospector, was one of Niles's outfit, wasn't he?"

"Sure was," Niles panted. "He double-crossed us. Zeb Quale used to come up to the ranch house to talk with Niles, who he thought was Willis Diebold, the son of his old friend. He showed Niles a chunk of the ore, and Niles found out somehow he'd made a map of the claim and meant to give it to Les Rutherford. Niles knew the strike was worth a fortune, but Quale wasn't sure of what he had—thought maybe it might be just a shallow pocket. He kept the exact location under his hat. So Niles set Ander to get in with him and find out what Quale knew. Ander looked to be an honest old-timer with his gray hair and whiskers, and Quale trusted him on Niles's say-so. He took Ander to the claim so's Ander could check it out."

"And that's when Ander killed him," Ki stated.

Jessie glanced at Ki. "But Quale was killed by that cougar!"

Ki shook his head. "No, Ander must've used somthing to make it look like a cougar attack. And he used the same method later on Lester Rutherford. Remember Matt Beemis describing how the front of Quale was torn to shreds, mauled face to foot? And Eve said that reminded her of the way her father looked when he was brought in? But that's not how a cougar kills. A cougar grasps its prey with its claws, hugging while it snaps the neck with its jaws. That's how the heifer was killed, and it should've tipped me off then."

177

"Smart o' you," Thayne said. "Yeah, Ander had a cougar forepaw stuffed and mounted on a handle. Dunno what become of it, now's Ander's dead. Anyhow, Ander cashed in Quale. But he didn't come back to Niles. He hightailed out of the country. But he come back, after he'd shaved his whiskers and dyed his hair. Niles was almighty smart, too, and spotted him right off. He set the boys to tail him. Anders was slippery and the boys couldn't catch him. Niles knew he was slippin' out high-grade ore and sellin' it below the border, but it weren't till we drove a herd of Anvil cattle south that we finally run into Ander, almost accidental-like."

"Of course!" Jessie exclaimed. "When we ran into Eve that first morning, Ki, you recall her telling us she was on the lookout for her foreman and his crew, who'd gone chasing rustlers. Anders must've been smuggling a load of ore southward, too, and had to turn back when he crossed paths with the rustlers."

"That's why he was heading north," Ki added.

"Well, some of the boys chased after him, caught up with him by Malazo Peak. You know how that ended." Thayne's eyes closed, but opened almost immediately. "Uh-huh, and I'm ended too . . ." His eyes closed wearily once more. They did not open again.

By now Matt Beemis and Eve Rutherford had joined Jessie and Ki. "Jessie," Beemis asked, "what made you suspect Diebold—I mean, Niles—was Quantrell?"

"Mud," Jessie replied. "Mud on his boots."

"Huh?"

"When Eve and I visited the Double Diamond ranch house to discuss a roundup, it had just finished raining. Niles, posing as Diebold, was sitting in a chair. From where I sat I had a good view of the inner sides of the high heels of his riding boots, and they were caked with fresh mud. Now Diebold was supposed to be a cripple. It struck me strange for a man who couldn't walk to have fresh mud on the inside of his boot heels, and it set me to wondering. His telegram helped, too."

"How's that?" Eve asked.

Jessie took out the piece of yellow message paper that she had torn off the pad in the telegraph office. "Thayne had just finished writing a message to be wired when I got to the telegrapher's. So I took this sheet, the next sheet on the pad, and lightly ran a soft pencil over it, so that the graphite would show the indentations of his writing. See? The message itself is perfectly innocent—he was wiring a buyer in El Sabinas to meet his part of the roundup herd. What's important is that his handwriting matched the handwriting on the note Shukka supposedly sent you, Ki, and on the warning note you received, Matt, from Quantrell."

"Y'mean the note that read 'stay out of malazo country you ain't wanted here and you aint got a chance in an hundred to git out alive we ain't fooling'?" Beemis asked.

"That's right. What made me keep the note was the odd wording. It appeared to be an illiterate scrawl, but no illiterate would ever use that construction '*an* hundred' instead of '*a* hundred.' Only a presumptuous man would use '*an*' that way. So, right there the writer slipped a mite. Didn't seem much, but it meant a lot to Shukka, the way things turned out, and saved me wasting time trying to tie him in as the outlaw leader."

Eve shook her head in admiration. "You certainly don't miss a trick, Jessie."

"That try at the payroll holdup on the trail to town helped link things to Niles, too," Jessie added. "It showed somebody in the Quantrell outfit had means of learning a considerable amount about the Lazarus Mine Company's business. Well, after I sent the wire and had lunch in town, I had a conversation with the mine superintendent, and learned that Niles, as Diebold, was friends with him and owned some stock in the Lazarus."

Beemis broke in to ask, "You figured that salt cart driver was Ander, the prospector?"

"Yes, after you told me the story of Zeb Quale's death. The man who was driving the cart had his hair died black and not long before had shaved off a heavy beard he'd been wearing for years. And I figured Ander to be the only man besides Quale who knew where that high-grade ore was coming from. I'd already decided it didn't come from the Lazarus Mine. The outlaws were too desperately anxious to keep a specimen from getting a close examination. Ander would dig out a cartload of ore, slip across the valley at night with the ore covered with a layer of salt, then amble down to Mexico as a salt peddler, and nobody who happened to see him would think anything of him or his load."

"Well, I certainly didn't," Eve admitted. "Where is the find?"

"On your land. We'll show you where. Naturally, that's why Niles wanted to get hold of the Anvil. He knew the gold ledge was here somewhere, but not exactly where. So he satisfied himself with cleaning the Anvil of livestock, knowing that if you kept losing, you wouldn't be able to meet your obligations and would have to go out of business. Then he'd buy up the Anvil and the ledge with it."

180

"Well, I guess there's nothing more for us to do now but keep an eye on the outlaws and Shukka's bunch, and wait for the sheriff," Beemis said.

"Where is Sheriff Gillette, anyway?" Eve asked.

"Yeah," Ki remarked, "there's never law around when you need it." Nor, as far as he was concerned, would there be any more hunters after that cougar. She was no man-eater, and if the cat downed a few cows for food, she was welcome to them after the help she'd given. Besides, although cougars had long been blamed for depleting herds, in fact their culling of old or injured animals appeared to enhance the herd's well-being. Truly the cougar was, as the Indians called it, "the spirit of the mountains." It was a spirit Ki had to admire, living on this day and hopefully into tomorrow in the wilds of America and in the hearts of those who wished it so.

Jessie, unaware of what Ki was thinking, glanced at Eve Rutherford and Matt Beemis. They stood close, smiling at each other as if they were seeing into a future that was bright and golden. Jessie's gaze shifted then. The vampire god, Quetzalcoatl, still crouched there on his pedestal, still smiled his cruel smile as he stared with wicked, greedy eyes over the cavern. Was he, she wondered grimly, lusting for the fresh, bright red blood that ran in tiny rivulets over the cavern floor?

Watch for

LONE STAR AND THE TRAIL OF MURDER

124th novel in the exciting LONE STAR series
from Jove

Coming in December!

*If you enjoyed this book,
subscribe now and get...*

TWO FREE

A $7.00 VALUE–

If you would like to read more of the very best, most exciting, adventurous, action-packed Westerns being published today, you'll want to subscribe to True Value's Western Home Subscription Service.

Each month the editors of True Value will select the 6 very best Westerns from America's leading publishers for special readers like you. You'll be able to preview these new titles as soon as they are published. *FREE* for ten days with no obligation!

TWO FREE BOOKS

When you subscribe, we'll send you your first month's shipment of the newest and best 6 Westerns for you to preview. With your first shipment, two of these books will be yours as our introductory gift to you absolutely *FREE* (a $7.00 value), regardless of what you decide to do. If

you like them, as much as we think you will, keep all six books but pay for just 4 at the low subscriber rate of just $2.75 each. If you decide to return them, keep 2 of the titles as our gift. No obligation.

Special Subscriber Savings

When you become a True Value subscriber you'll save money several ways. First, all regular monthly selections will be billed at the low subscriber price of just $2.75 each. That's at least a savings of $4.50 each month below the publishers price. Second, there is never any shipping, handling or other hidden charges—*Free home delivery*. What's more there is no minimum number of books you must buy, you may return any selection for full credit and you can cancel your subscription at any time. A TRUE VALUE!

A special offer for people who enjoy reading the best Westerns published today.

WESTERNS!

NO OBLIGATION

Mail the coupon below

To start your subscription and receive 2 FREE WESTERNS, fill out the coupon below and mail it today. We'll send your first shipment which includes 2 FREE BOOKS as soon as we receive it.

From the Creators of Longarm!

LONE STAR

Featuring the beautiful Jessica Starbuck
and her loyal half-American half-
Japanese martial arts sidekick Ki.